Something Left Behind

a novel by

Steve Reynolds

This is a work of fiction. Characters, corporations, institutions, organizations, and character locations in this novel are the product of the author's imagination. Any fictional similarity to real persons, organizations, or places is purely coincidental and unintentional.

Note for Librarians: A cataloguing record for this book is available from Library
and Archives Canada at www.collectionscanada.ca/amicus/index-e.html

Printed in Victoria, BC, Canada.

ISBN: 978-1-4269-1642-7 (soft)
ISBN: 978-1-4269-1643-4 (hard)

Library of Congress Control Number: 2009934468

*Our mission is to efficiently provide the world's finest, most comprehensive book publishing
service, enabling every author to experience success. To find out how to publish your
book, your way, and have it available worldwide, visit us online at www.trafford.com*

Trafford rev. 9/21/2009

 www.trafford.com

North America & international
toll-free: 1 888 232 4444 (USA & Canada)
phone: 250 383 6864 ♦ fax: 812 355 4082

for Peej

... in every way imaginable.

Acknowledgements

The work put into this story has truly been a labor of introspection and of love. Looking back, I realize it would never have been possible without the support, encouragement, guidance and love of others.

I must first thank my father, Lester, for providing me a unique and lasting impression of what breakfast is like with the town fathers at our local café. I am equally grateful to my mother, Emma Lou, without whose recipe for child rearing, I would not have found the perseverance to complete such an arduous task.

Further, I will forever be grateful to my daughter, Kasi, whose life has been a constant source of inspiration in my life. She serves as an endearing reminder that while I may not have always been the perfect father, I will nevertheless always be loved.

Finally, I am forever indebted to Tricia, who recently became my wife and who is in fact my very own "Amanda." With my undying love, I dedicate this story to her.

Completed August 20, 2001

Something Left Behind

Prologue

The afternoon sun was beginning to fade as Samantha Kane turned off the main highway onto the well-traveled, one-lane road that cut through the heart of the old cemetery. Without worrying she might fall victim to wind-swept hair, she rolled down the window of her Mercedes convertible and could immediately feel a distinct crispness in the late afternoon air. The cooler temperature was certainly not unusual for Illinois in October, but Samantha, known by those close to her as "Sam," had grown accustomed during the past few years to the warm, drier climate of Texas.

Although Sam spent her childhood enduring the cold winters of New England, she had quickly learned to appreciate the much warmer October days found in the South. Since graduating from college, she had lived in the Houston area for the past six years, where she was presently employed by a software development firm. She worked from her home, enjoying the comfort of her patio. It was there she would often sit with her laptop computer and write programs which would be used in the field of medical technology. Still, the coolness of this particular October afternoon was bringing back her childhood memories of autumn days gone by.

"Well, this place never changes," Sam mused aloud, as she slowly drove past grave after grave, each standing as a lasting memorial to some past inhabitant of the small town of Horton Grove. A rural community with a population of 982, Horton Grove was located six miles from the exact geographic center of the state, making it the closest town to bear that unique distinction. Yet this small claim to fame did little to change the fact that Horton Grove was the kind of place where nothing seemed to change from one year to the next. Sam felt certain this was still true for the year that had passed since she had last made this trip.

'What could make people spend their entire lives in just one place?' she wondered, as she headed for what had become a familiar corner of this town cemetery. 'More importantly,' she thought, 'what made him want to return to the place of his childhood, after escaping its ties and having lived his entire life elsewhere'?

Sam's thoughts referred to her father, Thomas Kane, who had died of a sudden heart attack three years earlier. Thomas became a college professor late in life and spent his last five years working at a small, private college in rural Colorado. His final days were spent teaching history, a subject that held a special fascination in him since his boyhood days spent in Horton Grove's small library.

Thomas Kane had lived alone after he and Sam's mother had divorced. It had been his wish, however, that upon death he be returned to his birthplace and laid to rest in the cemetery where his ancestors were buried. Today, Sam was once again making her annual pilgrimage to her father's gravesite.

As her car topped a slight rise, Sam could see that the graves were becoming newer. Since its creation over one hundred years ago, the Horton Grove cemetery had slowly grown from its original beginnings along the main highway.

Consequently, those who passed away in recent years were laid to rest further towards the back of the cemetery. As Sam continued the drive past the weathered gravestones, her memory confirmed she was getting close to her father's grave.

Although not exactly sure why she kept up this tradition, Sam continued to make this trip each year. Maybe it was because there was no one other than herself who cared. Certainly, Sam's mother did not care. In fact, her mother chose not to attend her father's funeral three years earlier. Still, who could blame her? When Sam was fifteen years old, her father had left home without any warning whatsoever. He simply left her mother a note one day that said he wanted out of their sixteen-year marriage. Just like that, her mother was without a husband. And Sam, who had remained with her mother, suddenly found herself without a father to give her the goodnight kiss which had been such an endearing father-daughter ritual as far back as she could remember.

"That which does not break you will make you stronger," her father had told her many times. Fact was, Sam never thought she would remember a fraction of all the things he said to her over the years. However, every time a situation warranted—and usually when she least expected it—she would hear her father's words echoing inside her head. Each time a small affidavit of advice crept in, it was almost as if he had somehow known what pearl of wisdom she would need at that exact moment in her life. Although slightly annoyed at the proverbial thought that she might very well have 'become her parents', still she smiled, recognizing the strength that her father's wisdom continued to bring to her life even after his death.

Rather than diminishing with the passing years, Sam's memories of childhood and of her father seemed to come back stronger each time she returned to the old cemetery. It was on the day of his funeral she had made the decision to return here each year. Perhaps it was her way of bringing more meaning to his life—a life that she never fully understood. Or perhaps she hoped it would somehow bring closure to the unanswered questions that still plagued her—questions regarding her father's choice years before to live his life alone.

For whatever reasons, Sam remained faithful to the promise she had made to herself and dutifully returned to this place each October on the anniversary of his death. And each time she came, she said a prayer, laid a single rose on his grave, and tried to remember the "good times" when they were still a family in the traditional sense—a time when they had lived together in New England. This was to be a quick visit, and she was not expecting today to be any different than her previous visits.

Sam gently brought the car to a stop near the end of the narrow road. She saw her father's grave now, inconspicuous with its small monument and located under a lone oak tree that had now lost its leaves in advance of the pending winter. Sam knew there was probably less than an hour of daylight remaining. Still, she elected to remain behind the wheel of the car for a few minutes more and reminisce. Her mind wandered back to a time when as a twelve-year-old, she stood beside her father in this same cemetery on the day of her grandfather's funeral. She remembered thinking then how odd it was that her father did not cry. After all, she most certainly would have cried had it been her daddy who died!

As her thoughts continued to wander, Sam remembered a day three years earlier when she stood under that same oak tree the day her father was buried. She suddenly recalled that even in her grief she, too, had not cried when her father was lowered into the ground.

'Like father, like daughter' Sam now thought. As each year came and went, that simple analogy seemed to manifest itself more and more.

Suddenly, Sam's thoughts were sidetracked when she realized there was something lying on top of her father's gravestone. From inside the car, it was impossible to determine exactly what it was. Sam opened the door and stepped out of the car. The old oak tree was a short walk from the road and Sam immediately headed toward it, trying with every step to identify the item that now held her curiosity.

With the passing of each season, the oak tree had become more weathered, slowly losing its battle to outlast the graves that surrounded its widely spread branches. As Sam neared her father's grave, she could see what now appeared to be a small bouquet of flowers lying across the top of the gravestone. In the final steps, she could see that it was a bouquet of violets, freshly cut, and beautifully accented with a perfect touch of Baby's Breath.

Staring at the freshly cut flowers, which suggested to her they were placed there earlier that day, Sam tried to imagine who might have left them. 'It might have been an old acquaintance from Dad's childhood,' she thought. While she could not remember their names, Sam did recall that a few of her father's childhood friends had attended his funeral. Other than perhaps one of these classmates from long ago, no one else came to mind. Yet, this simple bouquet of violets somehow seemed to suggest a deeper meaning than that of a classmate's respect.

And so it was, a father whose life Sam never fully understood continued to surprise and confuse her, even after his death. Sam had always been certain that her father's life was much sadder than most, especially after he left her and her mother. It was then he had become more withdrawn, more so than she ever remembered him being during her childhood.

With the sunlight almost gone, Sam dutifully laid her single rose across the grave. She silently said a prayer, asking God to bring peace and tranquility to Thomas Kane's soul. As she turned to leave, she looked once more at the bouquet of violets. Amidst thoughts of who the unknown visitor might have been, Sam gently removed one of the small flowers from the bouquet, walked back to her car, and left with the expectation that another year would pass before she would return again.

But for now, Sam had once again kept the promise she had made to herself. However, with the discovery of a lone bouquet of freshly cut violets, Sam found herself leaving this time with more questions than when she had arrived.

Chapter One

Winter had come early this year to Preston Falls, Colorado, and with it a total snowfall well above the average. While snow was no stranger to this rural mountain community, the additional precipitation this winter had all but cut off the town from the rest of the county. Quietly tucked away some twenty miles off Highway 139 north of Grand Junction, Preston Falls was near the south entrance to Douglas Pass. The towering mountains that surrounded this small but well-kept town served to create a weather phenomenon each winter whereby its citizens could expect to see over twice the average snowfall of the entire state.

But this year had been particularly brutal, with the seasonal expectation having already been achieved by the third week of January. The town fathers who met each weekday morning for coffee at Mandy's Café on Main Street predicted that the town had a real shot at breaking the snowfall record for a single season. At the very least, they believed Preston Falls had already experienced more snow this season than they could ever recollect seeing during any single winter during their lifetimes, record or not.

"Well, this is a record that I for one do not look forward to breaking," Mark Benton concluded, as he worked through his morning ritual of eggs, bacon, and hash browns. Mark, a twenty-eight year old English professor at Mountain View College, was the only young person at the old-timer's table.

With the population of Preston Falls doubling every fall and winter as five hundred or so students arrived to attend Mountain View, the resident population tended to give the young foreign arrivals their space. Although most Preston Falls folks were very private people and were inclined to shy away from outsiders, they nevertheless appreciated the revenue the college brought to their small community. It was a balance that seemed to work, as the students themselves tended to spend their free time experiencing the many outdoor attractions for which the Colorado mountains were famous. Quite frankly, Mandy's Café was simply not on their list of landmark venues.

Mark, however, was the exception to this rule. He had grown up in Preston Falls. For forty-two years, his father owned and operated the small hardware store three doors down from Mandy's Cafe. Mark's mother had spent most of her life teaching third grade at Preston Falls Elementary School. By default, this local lineage had bought Mark both the respect of the town and a seat each morning at this sacred table in a rear corner of Mandy's Café. Although he was younger than the others who sat around the table that morning, he was after all one of their own.

"What would you know about records?" barked George Vogel. George was Preston Falls's one and only retired postmaster, and it was a distinction he seldom let others forget. To hear George tell it, there were no mail deliveries in Preston Falls before he was postmaster. None of course except those made by Pony Express.

"Why, I can remember the winter of '47 when I carried a snow shovel with me on my mail route, digging through piles of the white stuff every step of the way!"

"Here we go again with another damn 'I can remember when…' story," Bob Tyler hastened to interject. Bob was probably George's oldest and closest friend. Perhaps it was because of this longtime relationship that Bob was generally the only one brave enough to put George in his place. "If you've told that story once, George, you've told it a million times!"

"Yes and every time 'ol George tells it, the mail route grows longer and the snow gets deeper!" Mark added with an infectious smile that was always contagious to those around him.

With Mark's remark, everyone feasted on a hearty round of laughter at George's expense. It seemed that this was the very point of daily congregation—to poke fun at one of their own. No one was immune; the light-hearted ridicule would simply gravitate from one to another, as years of personal history were roasted over well-meaning coals of camaraderie.

Mark was only twelve when his father first allowed him to join this informal group. He had told Mark that it was a ritual for old friends to drink coffee and 'tell lies to each other.' During the years after his parents had lost their lives in a car accident near Colorado Springs, Mark had come to know that these gatherings each morning were really all about preserving time. Most of these men were now retired and were facing the inevitable that is common to all. With each passing year, the group seemed to lose yet another of its members. Nevertheless, the memories of those now gone were never forgotten... not inside Mandy's Café, and especially not at *this* table. There was seldom a morning that went by without someone recalling, "say, do you remember when…" with everyone reaching the unanimous conclusion that, yes, that person was just about the finest person that had ever lived in Preston Falls. And most certainly, they would always agree, there would never be another person like that one.

With everyone still taking shots at George's 'I remember when' story, Mark, having now finished his breakfast and his third cup of coffee, rose from the table. "It's that time again, boys," Mark said. He began to search for his own winter coat amidst the cornucopia of seasonal coats, hats, scarves and gloves that adorned the wall hooks behind them. "I know that if I don't get out of here now, you'll all be trashing me next! And if you do, I'll be forced to defend myself with a vengeance!"

"Hell, boy, by the time you get the snow scraped off the windshield of your truck, these guys will be all over the fact that you're still single!" quipped Martin Dobbs, owner, manager, and sole popcorn-maker at the movie theatre located across the street from Mandy's. Since movies were only shown on the weekend, Martin spent most weekdays sitting inside Mandy's Café. Because of this longtime routine, he had achieved the reputation of being the one person who knew more about what was going on in Preston Falls than anyone else.

"That's the damn truth," added George, who now saw this as the perfect opportunity to shift the fun from his doorstep to someone else's.

"Why am I not surprised?!" Mark countered. "You guys should just be grateful I came back home after six years away at college. Otherwise, who would you have to gang up on other than your tired old selves?" Having once again left them with that famous Benton smile, Mark dutifully departed Mandy's Café for another day of teaching younger people the merits of writing while exercising proper, grammatically correct English.

Mark quickly brushed the snow from the windshield of his GMC Jimmy, put the vehicle into four-wheel drive, and headed north along the only road out of Preston Falls. Mountain View College, a small liberal arts and general studies institution founded some twenty-two years earlier, was located three miles outside of town, along the banks of the East Salt River. Its small, picturesque campus was framed on three sides by mountains that seemed to protect its inhabitants from the outside world. Though small and ever struggling to survive the lure of the larger universities, Mountain View continued to draw in just enough serious-minded students each year to support itself and the lives of its small group of faculty and staff.

Like most other schools, office space seemed to always be at a premium at the college. When Mark had returned home to Preston Falls three years earlier and had accepted the low-paying teaching position in the English department, he was told there was no office space available within his department. Consequently, Mark was forced to set up shop in a remote office located on the basement floor of Riggins Hall. While this move put Mark two floors away from the others who comprised his academic department, he found himself beside a couple of very friendly colleagues who made up the college's small history department.

Truth be known, Mark actually preferred the company of the two history professors over that of his own department faculty. The English professors at Mountain View had all written an assortment of fictional and non-fictional literary works, which helped further solidify their positions at the college. Mark, on the other hand, was still maturing as a teacher. By standards imposed by his colleagues, he had yet to publish anything of consequence. After three years at Mountain View College, he had come to believe this lack of expected publishing was a point of disappointment to the rest of his academic department. 'Publish or perish' seemed to be the key to tenure.

However, it wasn't that Mark didn't think about and hope for successful writing. Fact was, he often thought about publishing 'the great American novel.' He always believed that a truly great romantic story was lying dormant within of him, just waiting to be put onto paper. Yet another part of him believed the world already had enough dime-store romance novels. Consequently, the book remained unwritten.

Mark remembered how his mother would spend hours on end sitting on their front porch swing reading romance novels. Mark also remembered how his father had always referred to those same books as "literary pulp." His mother remained undaunted, however, by her husband's literary criticisms. She would simply smile and continue her reading. She seemed to find the deepest joy reading one teary-eyed story after another.

Like his mother, Mark, too, had spent many hours reading what others had written about love. He had often thought 'I wish I had said that...', and recurrently wished he could find a love as meaningful as those described in the novels he read. Still, Mark's own romantic relationships as a student in high school and in college had all been short-lived. Typically, the more serious the girl would become, the more he wanted out of the relationship. He was often accused of being unable to make a serious commitment. In Mark's mind, however, he remained hopeful the 'right' girl would eventually come along.

Mark's few feeble attempts at writing a romance novel had failed miserably. He had since come to the conclusion that he had yet to understand love; therefore, it was impossible for him to write about it. He also realized that reading all the great love stories and romantic poetry in the world would not teach him the true meaning of love. Mark resigned himself to the fact that if true love was ever meant to happen in his life, it would undoubtedly happen when he least expected it. All the analysis in the world could do nothing to make it happen any sooner than was destined.

Mark turned the Jimmy into the entrance of the college and slowly made his way down the main road that looped through the small campus. This morning, he could not help but notice that the wall of plowed snow lining both sides of the road had grown another foot as a result of the snowplows overnight. If the temperature did not warm above freezing, giving the plowed snow a chance to melt, it might eventually be piled higher than his truck.

That thought gave Mark an uneasy feeling. He always thought of himself as a closet claustrophobic. It was just another one of those personal things he kept to himself; it would not be a pretty picture if Mark's weaknesses or sensitivities became public knowledge among the old-timers who graced Mandy's Café each day.

He laughed at the thought of being a closet Claustrophobic. "Now that's an oxymoron, if there ever was one!" Mark exclaimed aloud. Like 'jumbo shrimp' and 'civil war,' the occasional absurdity of the English language never ceased to amuse Mark. He often challenged his students to ponder such gems as "why aren't the words 'abbreviation' and 'monosyllabic' just a little bit shorter?", "why isn't there another word for 'thesaurus'?", "why isn't 'palindrome' spelled the same backwards as it is forward?", and "why isn't 'phonetic' spelled the way it sounds?"

'Words… life's ultimate amusement,' he thought. As a professor of English, Mark sometimes wondered if he was in the wrong profession, since much of the very language he taught often made very little sense.

Mark turned into the snow-filled parking lot beside Riggins Hall and brought the truck to a stop. Gathering his briefcase full of student essays graded the night before, he cautiously traversed the icy sidewalk, entered the building, and proceeded downstairs to his office. As was usual during the winter months, Mark was welcomed by the seeming absence of heat in his little corner of the basement. Having grown accustomed to this phenomena—known by the college maintenance department as the-heat-is-working-just-fine—Mark had worn a pullover sweater specifically for this very reason.

A quick check of his daily schedule confirmed that today, Thursday, January 20, 2000, Mark had only one class to teach, a class on composition which was not scheduled until after lunch. Because of this light schedule, Thursday's this semester were Mark's favorite day. He quickly turned to his computer in an attempt to catch up on e-mails sent by his students, his colleagues, and, occasionally, an old friend from his days at Colorado State University. As the e-mail streamed into his desktop application from a server located elsewhere on campus, Mark noticed immediately that one was from old Martha Simmons… *Dr. Martha Simmons, Chair, Department of English Studies* to be exact.

'Damn!' Mark thought. 'I wonder what that crazy old woman wants *this* time.' Just last week, she had wanted him to chair a curriculum committee. The week before that, she had expected him to pick up an extra class next spring, so that she could take a 'much needed' vacation. And the week before that... 'Who even remembers?!' he thought in disgruntled agony.

Deciding it would serve no purpose to prolong the inevitable torture that was surely being bestowed upon him, Mark clicked open the e-mail from his academic leader and read the following:

Professor Benton: An office space has vacated on the second floor of Riggins Hall contiguous to the Department of English Studies...

'Who the hell uses the word "contiguous" inside these forty-eight states?' Mark mused. He made a note to compliment Ms. Martha on her munificent verbosity at their next staff meeting.

...It is therefore in the best interest of our department that you move from your current office in the basement floor, Riggins Hall, Room 038, to the second floor of same, Room 212, as soon as possible. Please be advised that you are being asked to bring all of the furniture from your old office with you, since Room 212 has, at present, no furniture. You should seek the assistance of campus maintenance personnel with the moving of your furniture. I will expect to see you moved by Monday morning.

At first thought, the idea of moving did not bother Mark, nor did the thought of doing so quickly during the next few days. However, the thought of moving next door to the department chair herself sent a shiver down his spine. He had grown accustomed to the security found in the secluded bowels of the basement and to the light friendships that had evolved among its politically inert inhabitants. He liked the fact that he could come and go as he pleased, without falling victim to Ms. Martha's watchful eye and unforgiving scrutiny.

Still, Mark had been at Mountain View College long enough to realize that it would be an exercise in futility to even try to argue his disappointment with the aged department chair. Her tenured rule was supreme and her decisions were, without exception, final.

With a sense of purpose now forced upon him, Mark knew what must be done. He dutifully called the maintenance department. The call was answered by Charlie, who staffed the phone most days. Charlie agreed to send over two workers with a freight dolly to move Mark's desk, chair, filing cabinet, and four bookcases to his new office upstairs.

Mark printed out a note to his 1:00 o'clock English composition class, dashed up three flights of stairs, and posted the note on the door of his classroom. This hastily prepared notice declared that today's class had been unexpectedly cancelled and that assignments due today would be collected on Monday.

Next, Mark donned his coat and trudged through the snow to the small campus bookstore. Since the bookstore also served the campus as a combination convenience store and post office, one could always find a few empty boxes there, boxes necessary for moving four bookcases full of textbooks.

Mark was glad to see that the boxes available in the bookstore were appropriately small. He had learned over the years that there was nothing on the face of the earth heavier than a box full of books. Breaking down each box flat, he was able to carry fourteen boxes back to the basement of Riggins Hall.

Mark had barely finished packing the fourth box, when two workers from the maintenance department arrived. Working together in practiced unison, they quickly packed the remainder of Mark's books, as well as other assorted office paraphernalia, and began the move to the second floor. The workers moved the boxes first, setting each of them to one side of the new office. Next, they moved the bookcases up the stairs to Mark's new second floor office. When the workers left to bring up the remaining pieces of furniture, Mark began unpacking the boxes, placing the books back into the bookcases in the same systematic order as before. It appeared as though this whole exercise would take less than a couple of hours at the most to complete.

As Mark continued arranging his books, the workers brought in his desk, chair, and finally his file cabinet. As the file cabinet was being brought in, one worker handed Mark a dusty manila envelope. Mark took the envelope without any thought. The slightly crumpled hand delivered envelope seemed to contain a good bit of material.

"Hope you didn't miss this too much," the worker said referring to the old envelope. "We found it behind your file cabinet. From the amount of dust on it, I'd say it has been there quite awhile!"

"Thanks," Mark answered gratefully. "I've been known to lose student essays on more than one occasion! Of course, when I do lose papers, I feel obligated to give the students an automatic "A", so they never seem to mind."

"I wouldn't think they'd mind!" replied the other worker, who had unhitched the dolly from the cabinet and was now preparing to leave. "Give us a yell, Doc, if we can do anything else for you."

Although Mark did not possess a doctorate degree, it was not uncommon for an occasional student or employee to refer to him as "doctor." At first, Mark would correct them. However, over time, he rather liked the sound of it and eventually quit correcting the well-intended mistake.

"And g-o-o-o-o-d luck!" one worker said slowly over his shoulder as they left. Mark knew the worker was eluding to the fact that he was now situated in the immediate proximity of old Ms. Martha. What Mark needed was more than luck; what he needed was another office located somewhere far away from his boss! He was already wondering how long it would be before he could move back away from her watchful eyes.

Mark spent the remainder of the day settling into his new home away from home. As if to comply with some universal mandate requiring visual proof of a professor's knowledge and ability to teach, he hung his two college degrees on the wall behind his desk. Next, knick-knacks were strategically dispersed about the room. Each was a trophy of some bygone place or event, with meaning known only to Mark, not necessarily to those who would see it.

With the mess for the most part now gone and some semblance of order restored to his professional life, Mark scanned the room with hollow approval, knowing already that he would miss his basement colleagues. As he looked about his new home, his eyes fell upon the old manila envelope now resting atop the last pile of papers and magazines on the corner of his desk. He could not help but wonder which papers, lost months earlier, were inside the dusty envelope. They were probably from his Creative Writing 331 class held nearly two years ago. What a fiasco that had been! The final written assignment required that each student submit a fictional novelette. Eighteen papers were turned in on time; he knew this because he had personally counted the papers before slipping them into a manila envelope. However, that weekend, as he prepared to grade them, the envelope was nowhere to be found. He could not find them at home, in his office, or even under the seat of his Jimmy, where items that fell from the seat had a tendency to hide. After hours of searching, he just assumed he had dropped the envelope between his office and the parking lot and that it had ended up in the trash somewhere.

Mark picked up the freshly resurrected envelope and gently blew the few remaining dust balls from the outside. He opened the metal clasp that loosely held down the top flap, reached inside, and pulled out the first piece of paper his fingers found. As the single sheet of paper was pulled from the envelope, Mark could see that this material was *not* his long lost class assignments.

Although Mark had read thousands of pages of literature over the years, had graded countless papers written by his students, and had himself written hundreds of pages in pursuit of his own education, he knew what he now held in hands had a meaning unlike anything he had seen before. What Mark did not know, however, was that this single piece of paper pulled from a dusty, somewhat crumpled manila envelope would forever change his life.

Chapter Two

am Kane spoke dryly into the portable phone, as she moved about her home watering numerous varieties of houseplants, many in seemingly desperate need attention.

"No, Mother, you are *not* going to be a grandmother anytime soon. You do realize, don't you, that I actually have to meet someone, first, who I *want* to marry, *before* I allow him to impregnate me? And the last time I checked, I had not met anyone I wanted to marry." With each passing year, Emily Kane was becoming more relentless regarding the subject of her daughter and grandchildren—more specifically, the distinct *lack* of grandchildren.

"You know what I mean," Sam's mother replied dryly. "I am only reminding you that the longer you wait, the more the good ones get taken. And each time a good one gets grabbed up, someone else is throwing a reject back into the pool!"

'Why do I even bother?' thought Sam. It is the same conversation every month. A person could set their biological clock by it. "Can we just change the subject?" she asked. "I promise to keep you apprised of my social successes immediately as they occur."

Undaunted, Emily Kane continued. "Well, it's just that you are nearly thirty years old, and if you don't hurry…"

"I *beg* your pardon," Sam interjected. "I am only twenty-eight years old; I'll be twenty-nine next month—*not* thirty!

Tell me, Mom, is it a universal tenet that mothers make their unmarried daughters feel older than they really are?!"

"Fine," her mother said abruptly. "If you are determined to end up with some divorced man who already comes with a couple of kids, far be it for me to stand in your way. In the meantime, know I love you, dear. Sunday dinner will be ready at six o'clock sharp. Try *not* to be late this time."

"I love you, too, Mom," Sam said, as she watered a flourishing fichus plant strategically placed to catch the afternoon sunlight that flooded one corner of her living room. "I'll try real hard to be on time. We certainly wouldn't want those mashed potatoes to get cold."

"And call your grandmother once in awhile," Emily added in a tone that sounded more like a reprimand than a reminder.

"I *will*, Mother. Talk to you again soon. Bye." With that, Sam concluded the daily ritual of assuring her mother, who lived only a few miles away, that all was well and that every man she encountered was being dutifully screened as both a candidate for marriage and as a potential father to Emily's unborn grandchildren.

For some inexplicable reason, Sam had been in one of her moods all day, and the phone call from her mother had not improved her disposition in the least. It always seemed that whenever Sam found herself feeling like this, she would resort to menial household chores, hoping the monotony of these tasks might chase away the blues. Today, however, this strategy did not seem to be working.

Having now watered her plants for the first time in at least two weeks, Sam began to dust the bookshelves that lined three walls of her living room. She moved one thing after another, meticulously dusting where each piece had rested.

As she dusted, her hands fell upon a small picture frame resting on one of the top shelves. She stared at it for a few moments, realizing that she had almost forgotten it was there. The frame contained a flower carefully pressed underneath the glass. During her last visit to the Horton Grove cemetery, she had taken this single violet from the anonymous bouquet found lying atop her father's gravestone.

As she looked at the flower for the first time in months, Sam found herself once again wondering who might have left those flowers at her father's grave. She slowly dusted the small frame, then placed it back on the top shelf. She took one last thoughtful look at the framed violet then went on about her dusting. Sam realized she had not told her mother about the flowers she found and made a mental note to tell her about them when they spoke tomorrow, even though her mother seldom showed any interest in talking about her father.

Mark Benton stared at the aging paper, finding it impossible to put down. After a few moments passed and his mind returned to the present, he carefully read it once more. Surprisingly, the words seemed more powerful the second time. Nothing Mark had read before seemed to convey the depth and emotion of the words he presently held in his hands. His education in literature told him these words contained a warmth and sensitivity which implied they were real, not fiction. And although he had no immediate proof, he felt certain that what he was holding were words written by someone obviously very much in love.

That thought now intrigued Mark. His mind raced to think that these words—intended only for the affection of another person's heart—were now being made known to a complete stranger. Mark read the words a third time.

"I loved you long before I met you.
I often wrote to you...
words that would wait years to find their way to you.

In finding you, I have now found myself.
Suddenly, I look forward to the rest of my life,
in a way never before imagined.
For me, you have defined the meaning of love.
You excite me so!

My life before was spent searching for you;
my life now revolves around you.

When we first met, you were friendly, helpful,
and you always smiled when you looked my way;
yet, you seemed to hold a part of you close inside.

Now, as our lives merge
and the love between us grows,
I see you opening your heart and soul.

I find myself anxious to be with you...
to watch and encourage what it is you open into
and who it is you become."

Mark laid the paper on his desk. He looked again at the aging envelope. It was obvious that inside this lost and forgotten package were many more papers—papers of an unknown origin.

"What is all of this?" Mark wondered aloud. Knowing that there was only one way to find out, he picked up the envelope and pulled out a second sheet of paper. As he read the words, his anticipation was quickly rewarded.

"I find myself wondering exactly when it is we reach middle age...
Someone once said that it is when
you go from looking good,
to looking good for your age!

I worry that it is when we start thinking about
all of the bad things that have happened in our lives,
instead of all the good things
that are yet to come.

Have you come so far in life
that your past keeps you from looking to the future?
Or, have you not yet come far enough
to embrace the hopes and dreams you hold dear?

Our love is changing us forever,
and in ways that promise there is so much more love to come.

Look at me; look to me.
I am everything you hope for
and you are my every dream."

Mark laid the second sheet of paper on top the first. The clock on the wall of his office showed that it was nearly two o'clock in the afternoon. He knew he had no choice; he had to read everything the envelope contained. There simply could be no stopping this now.

One by one, Mark Benton began to read the deepest secrets of a person he did not know. The words were written in the form of poetry and were written to a person who was never identified. He found himself not knowing whether to feel ashamed and guilty for violating something so very private or to allow himself the excitement of being given a glimpse of how true love must feel.

However, long before he could read everything the envelope contained, the sunlight began to fade from the one window in his new upstairs office. Mark knew it was time to pack up and head home for the day. It was nearly six o'clock and the breakfast eaten at Mandy's Café that morning had long since worn off. Carefully packing the old envelope into his well used and often overstuffed briefcase, Mark left his office feeling emotionally moved. He had stumbled upon something that had instantly captured his professional interest, as well as his personal curiosity and admiration.

Mark guided his four-wheel drive truck down the snow-covered streets of Preston Falls and thought about who the author of such eloquent and heart-felt words might have been. Although he had read nearly half of the envelope's contents, nowhere had there been any mention of who the writer was, or to whom the writer was addressing. Mark suddenly realized he could not even be sure if the author was a man or woman. This thought only served to further heighten his curiosity and desire to read more.

As if to acclaim the approaching darkness, the streetlights of Preston Falls began to flicker on in apparent random order. Driving past Mandy's Café, Mark could see it was already dark inside the small restaurant. The sign on the front door had been flipped to succinctly display the word "CLOSED."

Mark found himself wondering if he should even mention the discovery of the manila envelope to his elderly friends over breakfast the next morning. His immediate instinct was *not* to tell them. He was just not sure they were the sort of crowd who would appreciate the rarity and beauty of the words left behind in a crumpled manila envelope. Furthermore, they would probably not understand his sudden interest in a bunch of old love poems. That, of course, would be fodder for certain ridicule with the old-timers. Mark was not sure *he* even understood his immediate attraction to what had been found. He only knew that with every word he read, he felt deeply compelled to learn all he could about this touching love story.

Mark turned into the driveway of his small but adequate house located two blocks off Main Street. He dutifully trudged across the small front yard to check his mailbox, only to find a lone Western Auto sales flyer that had been hastily shoved inside. 'Hardly worth the walk,' Mark thought and headed inside.

With his coat, scarf, and gloves hung in the hall closet and his boots and shoes neatly placed on a foyer mat designed to absorb melting snow, Mark began his evening ritual. He turned on the evening news and while he cooked himself dinner, listened to the daily summary of national and world events. Knowing what was going on around the globe was more a requirement of his morning get-together at Mandy's than it was a requirement of his academic profession. "Did you hear what those damn oil ministers are doing now?" would be a typical question presented at the town father's morning soiree. Knowing the questions and commentary in advance served to keep Mark informed, which in turn, seemed to hold him in good stead with the group. Although they would publicly give him a hard time about being 'too young to know anything', Mark sensed that privately they valued both his opinion and the education they themselves lacked.

After eating dinner in record time, Mark settled into his living room recliner with the manila envelope resting on his lap. He pulled more papers from the old envelope and continued his reading.

"Her very presence in my life
Has touched my heart and soul.
Yet wanting her the way I do
Demands a heavy toll.

I cling to her shadow—unknown to her—
And treasure each passing day.
The words I long to speak aloud
Are words I cannot say.

The measure of her faith in me
Appears to have no bound.
My mind has become hopelessly lost
With feelings suddenly found.

She's given birth within my heart
A desire I've never known.
Yet her smile only heightens the pain I feel
Of living my life alone.

She's made me realize other loves
Were nothing more than whim.
And while my life has caught her eye,
Her life belongs to him."

"It *is* a man writing to a woman!" Mark exclaimed aloud, genuinely pleased that he had just solved the first piece of this endearing mystery.

While he had assumed this was probably the case, he could now better imagine the context of each poem. Up to this point, the writer had only referred to her as "you." It now also appeared that the woman was apparently involved with another man, much to the lament of the person writing the poetry.

Mark wondered if the woman was, at this point, even aware of the writer's love for her. Intent on learning more, Mark continued to read.

"While lost and feeling all alone
(forever, it would seem),
You brought a ray of light and hope
To an ever-darkening dream.

Your charm has captured my every breath;
Your smile, my empty heart.
Your touch transcends all time and space
As we spend our nights apart.

To feel your warmth, I lie alone,
And close my teary eyes.
I hear the words you spoke to me,
And pray they were not lies.

You know the love I have to give
Will make your life complete.
Yet you worry others will see you as
A failure and a cheat.

You've yet to learn, for all your years,
Love comes in many ways.
There are as many shades of love
As the morning sun has rays.

Your love for him need not die;
It's not a matter of choice.
It only means your heart can grow;
In our love you can rejoice.

To embrace the love I have to give
Will forever set you free
To leave a life that cannot grow
With someone who's not me."

'It would certainly seem that she was aware of his love,' Mark now surmised. He found himself secretly hoping the two would get together in the end. After all, a love this romantic had to prevail—it just had to!

As Mark read page after page, he failed to find any clues to the identity of either the man or the woman. The words inside the envelope were not in any obvious order. Consequently, Mark struggled to understand the writer's mood and context as it changed from one page to the next. Furthermore, there was no indication when any of the poems were written.

"I wonder how old this stuff is!" Mark exclaimed aloud. He continued to read, hoping for additional clues to the identities of the man and woman.

When Mark put down the last sheet of paper, he glanced at the clock on the fireplace mantel and saw that it was now nearly nine o'clock. He had now read the entire collection found inside the old envelope. There were ninety-two poems in all. While most were short in length, each had been rich in meaning and abundant in love. Even with each poem being read individually, perhaps out of order and out of context, there was an underlying message of love that touched a chord deep within Mark's own heart. He placed the manila envelope back into his briefcase, turned out the living room light, and headed off to bed. It had been, by any measure, a *very* long day.

As he lay in bed that night, Mark could not help but picture this loving couple in his mind. He imagined them young, with romance overflowing between them. He also tried to imagine the couple as they were today. Perhaps they middle aged, or, perhaps they senior citizens now, sitting on a porch swing somewhere, still holding hands and gazing as lovers do into each other eyes. Mark could even imagine children—or are they grandchildren?—running and playing in the front yard, while the man and woman sat on the swing and watched with loving eyes.

One of the last poems Mark had read that evening before retiring did seem to support his hope that the two fell in love, married, and lived happily ever after. The words referred to the couple's apparent upcoming marriage.

"I don't know where you came from,
Or why you chose to stay.
Still, the simple touch of your hand in mine
Means more than words can say.

All that I have ever been;
All I'll ever be
Shines within your loving eyes
When you smile and look at me.

My love for you begins and ends
Deep within my soul.
The passion you cause to rise within
Is beyond my will to control.

I long to shout the joy I feel,
And tell those who are near,
The one who loves me is no longer
An image in the mirror.

The pain I've known has gone away;
You mean the world to me.
I treasure the joy our love has brought-
A love meant to be.

Because of you I've come to know
The meaning of my life.
I now count moments as moments lost
Until you become my wife."

Mark nearly sat upright in bed. Assuming this couple might now be in their forties or fifties, he suddenly thought, 'What a wonderful present it would be if I could learn their identities, track them down, and give them back their words—words that were never intended to be seen by anyone other than themselves!'

His mind was racing. 'This could be easy! First, I need to find out who occupied my basement office prior to my arrival three years ago. Perhaps they wrote the poetry, or, received it from somewhere or someone, and would consequently know its origin. That previous occupant either hid the poems behind the file cabinet or the envelope accidentally fell there, where it has remained undetected for the last three or more years.'

Mark fluffed his pillow and lay down once again. 'What a story!' he thought. 'This could become the subject of a non-fiction article for a major magazine. Lord knows I could stand some national circulation and exposure! 'Ol Ms. Martha would have to throw a little literary respect my way then!'

As snow once again began to fall outside, Mark fell asleep that night and dreamed of critical acclaim and national fame. It was as if God was somehow trying to bury Preston Falls and at the same time bury the identities of a man and a woman whose love seemed as pure as the falling snow.

Chapter Three

s the alarm clock incessantly beeped the unwanted reality that morning had arrived, Mark Benton refused to believe it was time to get up. However, after a few minutes more of the relentless noise, he forced himself to turn off the alarm and head for the shower. His mind returned to the writings he had found the previous day. Because of this, Mark's morning routine proceeded within a new cloud of thought, resulting in his being ready to leave for work a full thirty minutes later than normal. Of course, "late" was a relative term in the small community of Preston Falls, Colorado.

With briefcase in hand, Mark stepped out into the bright morning sun. The snow had ended sometime during the night, and the clouds were all but gone. It appeared that Preston Falls had received an additional two inches of snow overnight. Mark started the engine of his truck and while the engine warmed up, turned to the task of brushing snow from the windows. He quickly completed this all-too-familiar task and drove to Mandy's Café for breakfast.

"You just about lost your seat, boy!" hollered George Vogel, as Mark entered the restaurant. "But, I made Marty pull up a chair from another table."

"You just *think* you made me," quipped Martin Dobbs. "Fact is, I just didn't feel like arguing with you this morning, at least not before I'd had my first cup of coffee."

"Thanks, George. I appreciate the way you look out for me," Mark said, as he flashed his smile across the room. Mark came to realize over the years that he somehow had become a surrogate son to George, although he was not quite sure why. He hung up his coat and joined the others at the overcrowded table.

"Running a little late this morning, aren't we?" George asked. "You wouldn't be holding out on us now, would you?"

"Holding out?" Mark asked. Of course, he *knew* what George meant. Mark's love life proved to be a constant source of intrigue and entertainment to those sitting around the table. Anyone being twenty-eight years old, college educated, employed, *and* single just did not seem quite right to this group. They made it a point to prod into Mark's private life every time the occasion warranted.

"Yeah, holding out!" echoed Bob Tyler. "You don't have some sweet young girl we don't know about boarded up at your place for the winter, now do you?!"

"You guys need to live vicariously through someone else for a while," Mark said, as Jenny Snyder—a fifty-two year old waitress by morning and local hairdresser by afternoon—delivered his usual breakfast. "Thanks, Jen," he added, amidst a background of laughter.

"You shouldn't waste big words like 'vicarious' on these tired old fools," Jenny cautioned Mark, as she refilled the coffee cups scattered about the table. "I doubt they even know what it means."

"Hey, I might be tired, and I might be old, but I ain't no fool!" Martin quickly offered in self-defense.

"You never married me, Martin Dobbs! And in my book," Jenny countered, "that damn sure makes you a fool!"

Suddenly, Martin had become the center of verbal abuse, taking the attention off Mark for the moment. Such moves were typical of this group's dynamics; no issue and no one was protected from its well-meant wrath. Even though Mark was glad to see fun poked elsewhere, he decided to jump in and save Martin any continued embarrassment.

"No, I'm not 'holding out'," Mark said with deliberate seriousness. "I was just up late last night reading some papers and had trouble getting myself around this morning."

As Mark quickly ate his breakfast, conversation at the table moved from Bob Tyler's snowplow, which happened to be on the fritz again, to George Vogel's bunions which never seemed to completely go away. Everyone was enjoying a third cup of coffee before Mark mentioned the "big" news from the previous day.

"Hey, I forgot to tell you guys! I moved out of the basement of Riggins Hall yesterday," Mark told the group. "An office became available upstairs and I was finally able to move in with my department."

"No more early lunches!" George cautioned with a grin. "You'll have to be on your best behavior from now on!"

"You're probably right," agreed Mark. "But, it is nice to finally be out of the basement office."

Suddenly, Mark became aware of the time and realized he needed to go. Leaving his usual two-dollar tip for Jenny, he rose to his feet. "This has been fun, guys, but I have got to get to work." As he headed for the door, Mark turned and added, "See you all on Monday."

"Don't expect me to save your seat again, boy," yelled George. "You just get your butt out of bed like the rest of us."

'Ah, yes,' thought Mark, 'the parting shot!' Mornings at Mandy's Café were somehow not complete without it. As he opened the front door of the café, he looked over his shoulder, gave them the famous Benton smile, and left. As he walked to his truck, Mark waved to Art Manning, snowplow driver extraordinaire, who was making what appeared to be his final pass down Main Street.

Still thinking about what he had read the night before made the drive to his new office seem shorter than usual. Mark was soon sitting at his desk, staring at the dirty, wrinkled manila envelope full of poignant words. It was time to solve the first piece of this newly found and intriguing mystery: specifically, the name of the person who occupied the basement office prior to his arrival at Mountain View College.

Mark picked up the telephone and dialed Rick Hastings. Rick had been teaching history at the college for the past three years and had been hired a few months prior to Mark's coming. Rick occupied the office adjacent to Mark's old basement office.

Rick answered the call in his usual fashion, "MVC History Department; Hastings speaking."

"Rick, this is Mark."

"Sorry, but you'll have to speak up!" Rick teased in a louder than normal voice. "You sound really far away. Where the hell are you?"

"You know *exactly* where I am," Mark replied. "I am two floors up, right next door to old lady Simmons herself.

You *have* to promise me that I still have a home away from home anytime I need it!"

"Sure, pal," Rick assured Mark. "Just bring your own Pepsi; I don't cater."

"No problem," replied Mark. "Listen, I have a history question for you this morning."

"Well, well, the great Mark Benton finally bows to my expertise!" Rick taunted good-naturedly. "Let's hear it, buddy."

"Okay," Mark began. "Well, I wanted to ask you about the history professor that you replaced three years ago. Do you remember his name?"

"Sure," Rick answered. "Dr. Thomas Kane. Why do you ask?"

"Didn't you tell me once that my office in the basement had previously housed a history professor who was no longer around?" Mark asked. "Was it Kane's?"

"Yes," Rick replied. "You were given Kane's office. I would have gotten it, except that, when I came, Kane's stuff was still in there. Consequently, I moved into the office next to his. Why do you ask, Mark?"

"Well, it's no big deal, really," Mark explained. "It's just that when the maintenance department moved me upstairs yesterday, an envelope was found behind my file cabinet. When I looked, it was nothing that belonged to me. It contains what appears to be notes of a personal nature. I thought it might be an appropriate gesture, if I mailed the material back to owner. Do you know where Kane is working these days?"

"All I can tell you is that he went back East somewhere," Rick recalled. "However, I know for a fact he isn't working."

"Really," Mark asked, "are you sure?"

"Oh, I'm sure alright," said Rick. "Mark, he died suddenly in his home here in Preston Falls—right in the middle of fall semester, a little over three years ago. Beyond that, all I remember is that his body was sent back East for burial, probably back to wherever it was he grew up."

What Rick had just revealed caught Mark totally by surprise. His dream of returning the poetry to a happily married couple was now gone. 'Well,' he quickly thought, 'it still could make a nice story if I returned these notes to his widow.'

"Do you, by any chance, happen to remember the name of Kane's wife?" Mark asked.

Rick thought for a long moment. "Well, come to think of it, that's exactly the reason it took so long to get his office cleaned out. Kane did not have a wife. Someone told me that he was single when he came to Mountain View and as far as I remember, he never married during the time he was here. There was a daughter, I think, from an early marriage, who showed up about a month after he died to claim his things. I never met her, though. She just showed up unannounced one weekend. When I came in the following Monday morning, all Kane's things were gone. Lester, over in security, told me Kane's daughter had come that Saturday and had cleaned out his office. A few weeks later, you showed up, moved in your things, and the cycle of collegiate office life continued."

"Well, do you know if Kane had a girlfriend?" Mark pressed, still struggling for a clue to the identity of the woman to whom Kane had written.

"Got me, pal," Rick replied. "I never met the guy. Like I said, he was gone before I got here."

"Well, thanks Rick for the information," Mark said gratefully. "I suppose these papers can probably be tossed. I just thought if anyone knew where the man might be, I could mail the envelope to him. But, seeing as though he died over three years ago, the effort certainly seems moot."

It was obvious to Mark he had reached a dead end. "Listen, I need to run. Talk to you later."

"Take care, pal," Rick said, "and don't become a stranger now that you are upstairs with the movers and shakers!"

"I won't," Mark assured him and hung up the phone greatly disappointed.

For late January, it was unseasonably warm and riding with the top down was a treat Sam could not resist on this particular Sunday afternoon. As the convertible pulled into her mother's driveway, Sam looked toward the sky. She knew that she would stay a couple of hours or more and she needed to decide whether or not to put the top back up on her car. Seeing no threat of imminent precipitation, she decided to leave it down and stepped out of the car.

The neighborhood was safe enough, populated by older retirees who preferred a more traditional lifestyle than that offered by retirement homes or villages. Here, they could enjoy their retirement, tending to their small track houses. As Sam looked up the street, she saw several elderly neighbors nurturing their tiny, well-manicured lawns and flowerbeds. Sam was glad her mother had located in this neighborhood.

It was close enough that Sam could quickly respond should her mother need her in a hurry.

Without knocking, Sam called out as she entered the small Cape Cod-style house. "Mom, are you home?"

"In the kitchen, dear," her mother answered. "Have you brought a guest with you or are you alone?"

'Well, that was about as subtle as someone yelling "Fire!" in a crowded movie theatre,' Sam thought to herself.

"I don't know of anyone in the Houston metropolitan area," Sam answered, "who *wants* to eat Sunday dinner with someone else's mother, so I had to come alone. I hope that was okay."

Emily walked from the kitchen into the living room and found her daughter looking at the many pictures adorning the mantel above the small fireplace. It was not a "real" fireplace, designed instead for fake gas logs. Still, with the pictures on the mantel, it added warmth that reminded Emily of her years in New England.

"Do you remember when we took this one?" Emily asked, picking up one of the small framed pictures and showing Sam. "It has always been one of my favorites."

Sam looked at the picture. The photograph was of her and her mother sitting outside an ice cream shop. It had been taken at the very instant they were both desperately trying to lick melting ice cream from the sides of their cones.

"Sure I do, Mom. I was twelve years old. We were in Bar Harbor, Maine, for Fourth of July vacation." Sam smiled, as she looked at the photograph that had captured this particular memory. "Leave it to Dad to catch us both with our tongues sticking out!"

"Yes, your father did have a sense of humor." With that single reference to Thomas Kane, Emily returned to the kitchen. "Come help set the table, dear."

Sam returned the picture to its original location on the mantel and followed her mother into the kitchen. The smell of dinner cooking on the stove always took Sam back to a simpler time—to a time when the world and all its problems seemed less complex. In Sam's current world, the smell of a well-balanced meal cooking was not something one should expect to find emanating from her kitchen. Her idea of a warm and nutritious meal was one that came from her microwave via her freezer.

As she began to place dishes and silverware on the small table in preparation for their meal, Sam thought perhaps now was as good a time as any to ask her mother's opinion regarding the flowers on her father's grave. She had wanted to talk to her mother about the violets since the day she returned from the cemetery. Until now, however, it never seemed like the "right" time to broach the subject.

"Mom," Sam began slowly, "do you remember when I got back from my trip to Horton Grove last October and you asked if everything was as it should be—I mean, with Dad's grave and everything?"

Emily looked up from the counter where she was busily preparing a fresh salad. "Yes," she answered cautiously, knowing that anytime a child attempted to qualify what they were about to say, it usually meant trouble. "Why?"

"Well, there was one detail I failed to mention. It is probably nothing and I'm not even sure why I bring it up now. It's just that it has sort of been nagging at me lately, so I thought I might as well mention it and see what you think."

"What is it, dear?" her mother asked. "You know how impatient I get when you beat around the bush about something. Come on, out with it!"

"Well, like I said, it's probably nothing. Nevertheless, when I visited the cemetery last October, I discovered that someone had left a small bouquet of flowers on Dad's gravestone. The bouquet seemed to have been freshly cut meaning they had probably been placed there shortly before I arrived. At first, I thought perhaps an old classmate had paid their respects. But the more I looked at the flowers, they just seemed to suggest something more. Anyway, I thought I'd mention it and see if you might know anything about it. I even thought that perhaps you sent them, since they were obviously laid there on the anniversary of his death, as opposed to Memorial Day, the more traditional day of remembrance."

Emily shrugged her shoulders in an outward gesture of indifference. "I wouldn't know anything about it. The flowers were not from me." Placing the last of the food onto the table, she then added, "Let's eat."

Sam dutifully sat down at the table. Emily bowed her head and, as a matter of routine, said a short but meaningful grace aloud. As the bowls of food passed between them, Sam tried a second time.

"So you don't have any idea where the violets might have come from?" she asked.

"Violets?" Emily asked. "You didn't mention that they were violets."

Sam now detected a distinct note of interest in her mother's voice. "Are violet's significant in some way?" she asked.

"I really couldn't say, without knowing who left them and why," Emily replied. "All I can tell you is that violets were your father's favorite flower."

"I never knew that," said Sam. "Why were they his favorite?"

"I'm not sure, really," answered Emily. "He just told me once that he preferred the simple beauty of violets over more traditionally romantic flowers, such as roses. The only problem, according to him, was that florists never seemed able to find fresh-cut violets. And it was for that reason he never bought me flowers."

Emily then smiled, as an image of her daughter suddenly came to mind. "I can remember one Saturday, when you were about four years old. Your father took you to the park so you could fly your new kite. Upon returning, you came running in, yelling for me at the top of your lungs as you raced through the house. When you found me putting away laundry upstairs, you proudly showed me a bouquet of wild violets that you and your father had picked. You said that you had found them growing along the bank of a brook that ran through the park. I can remember to this day how jealous I felt, as I smiled at you and told you how pretty they were. Secretly, I had wished that your father had picked those flowers for me instead of you."

Suddenly, the smile disappeared from Emily's eyes, replaced with a look of sadness Sam seldom saw. She reached across the table, placing her own hands upon the hands of her mother.

"I hope that someday, I will be as loving a mother to my own daughter as you have always been to me," Sam said.

"You are so sweet, dear, and I do love you," replied Emily, with a smile that seemed more an obvious effort to recompose oneself. "But, like I said, I can't be sure that the violets mean anything special. Still, violets are not a common flower that one can buy, as your father pointed out—especially in October. For someone to leave a bouquet of violets might very well mean there is some sort of significance. As far as who might have left them, though, I'm afraid I don't have a clue."

As the table was cleared and the dishes were washed and put away, Sam contemplated her mother's thoughts regarding the flowers. The more she thought about it, the more she tended to agree with her mother's guess that the violets did hold some sort of meaning. A short while later, as Sam prepared to leave for home, it was her mother brought up the subject once again.

"If the kind of flowers is significant," Emily conjectured, as they walked out onto the small front porch adorned with pots filled with flowers of numerous varieties, "and, if the date they were placed is also significant, then it begs another question. Did you notice flowers on your father's gravestone the previous years you traveled to the cemetery?"

Sam stopped abruptly, turning to face her mother. Her mind returned to those two previous occasions, only to quickly realize that her mother's question would not yield any additional clues.

"No, there were no flowers there during my past visits," Sam said, somewhat disappointed. "I'm sure I would remember if there had been."

"Well, sorry I can't be more helpful, dear," her mother replied. "If I were you, I wouldn't waste a lot of time trying to figure it out. I don't mean to speak ill of your father, but I never did understand the life he chose to live."

"You're probably right, Mom," agreed Sam. Then, changing the subject, she added "And dinner was great, as usual! Thanks for the fuss. See you next Sunday, right?"

"Goodbye, Dear," her mother called out after her. "Be careful driving home. And let me know by Thursday what you'd like to eat next Sunday and if you will be bringing a guest."

Sam dutifully waved, as she drove away. During the short ride home, her mind returned to what her mother had said regarding the violets. She still tended to agree that the violets probably held some special significance. Even so, Sam ultimately accepted her mother's advice not to worry about it and once again put the mystery out of her mind.

Chapter Four

inter in Preston Falls continued its course and during the next month, record snowfall continued to accumulate. By the first week of March, previous records had been broken and mountains of dirty snow could be seen piled up everywhere. With spring now approaching, local concern turned to the potential flooding hazards that record snowfalls tend to bring.

During the months that passed since discovering the envelope, Mark had read the poetry many times. Yet, he had done little more to uncover the identity of the mysterious woman. Once he learned of Thomas Kane's sudden death from his colleague Rick Hastings, the mystery seemed unsolvable. At least, it had seemed that way, until this particular Monday morning.

As Mark was taking his morning shower, the thought occurred to him that maybe—*just maybe*—his old friend George Vogel might be able to shed some light on the mystery. After all, George knew everyone in Preston Falls. Furthermore, George knew everyone who *ever* lived in Preston Falls. Still, Mark would have to be careful how he broached the subject. He was not willing to share the existence of the poetry with anyone just yet—at least not until he knew who the woman was and where she was.

Within the hour, Mark was sitting in Mandy's Café sipping his third cup of coffee. The conversation thus far had ranged from what was already being predicted as the "Great Snow Melt of 2000" to the president's chance of continuing his claim on the White House for another term.

"I hate to change the subject," Mark finally interjected, "but I got caught in a conversation over at Mountain View College last week, where the name of a previous faculty member totally escaped my memory. I suppose hanging around you old fools every morning is starting to adversely affect my memory. It must be true what they say about 'old-timer's disease'," Mark teased, in a tasteless reference to Alzheimer's disease. "Whatever it is you all have *is* contagious!"

"The hell you say!" rallied Bob, in defense of the aged group. "Tell us about the professor and we'll tell you his name."

"Well, he taught history at the college," Mark replied. "That is, until he died a little over three years ago. I know I heard the name back when I started, but I just can't seem to remember it now."

"I know who you are talking about." Bob said, as his memory began to process the information. "Just give me a minute and I'll spit it right out!"

George was quick to jump on Bob's inability to recall the name instantly. "That's *exactly* why you failed your civil service exam back in '53!" George concluded, obviously drawing on his years of employment as the postmaster for Preston Falls. "His name was Thomas Kane. His address was 917 Shannon. You know, the old Potter house—light blue with the black shutters. He subscribed to National Geographic magazine, he received USA Today every day except Saturdays and Sundays, and he seldom got any mail of a personal nature. Furthermore, if *my* memory serves me better than everyone else's, and it obviously does, he was an alumnus of the University of Illinois."

"For God sake, George, now you're making up shit!" said Martin. "How in the hell could you possibly know what college the man went to? He only lived in Preston Falls for a couple of years!"

"*Five* years, to be exact," George countered with professional precision. "And, I *know* he went to the University of Illinois because of all the college alumni mail that came his way."

'Good thinking!' Mark thought, knowing all too well the life-long alumni mail a college graduate is destined to receive.

"Well, there you go," replied Martin, giving George a look of total disgust. "Ask for a simple name and you get a complete biography!"

"I suppose you remember his shoe size, too!" Bob chided, bringing a new round of laughter to the table.

"Well, he *was* a tall man," replied George, determined not to be snookered by his peers. "I suspect he was a size twelve."

In an effort to keep the conversation from digressing any further, Mark quickly interjected his next question. "George, do you recall if he was married, or if he was seeing anyone during his stay in Preston Falls?"

"Kane was not married," George answered, "and, as best I can recollect, he was never seen in the company of anyone."

"Would it make any sense," Mark continued in a carefully constructed manner, "if someone over at Mountain View said that they thought Kane had a daughter? Apparently, a girl claiming to be his daughter came to the college and retrieved Kane's personal belongings a few weeks after his death."

George took a few extra moments on this particular question. Mark could sense that George was going back in his mind, trying to remember any personal mail Thomas Kane received during his five years in Preston Falls. At the same time, everyone else at the table had decided it was time to leave, especially since the current subject brought very little appeal to their collective curiosity. After routine goodbyes and several parting shots were exchanged, George turned back to Mark.

"Actually," George concluded, after a moments more thought, "that might make a lot of sense. Remember I said that Kane received very little in the way of personal mail?"

"Yes," Mark recalled.

"Well," George continued, "I don't remember any specific names or addresses, but I do recall that the personal items would always come from someone whose last name was also Kane. I think I just assumed that the sender was perhaps a brother and never gave it much thought. I suppose that person could have been a daughter—an unwed daughter."

George studied his young friend's face, as Mark began to digest what George had just said. "You have now fueled my curiosity," George said. "Why the sudden interest in a person you've never met?"

"To tell you the truth, George, it's all probably just a waste of time," Mark explained. "When I moved out of my old office several weeks ago, some personal notes were found behind a filing cabinet. I first thought I would try to return the papers to this Kane fellow, but I learned the man had passed away. Someone later mentioned he had a daughter, so I thought I might try to return the envelope to her."

"Well," George said, suddenly becoming less interested in the current subject of conversation. "I'm not sure I was much help."

"Well, I can understand not remembering exact names and return addresses from mail five years ago," Mark said, "but just knowing now that his daughter lived in Illinois might prove helpful."

"Who said anything about this other Kane living in Illinois?" George asked abruptly. "I said that he got mail from the alumni association at the University of Illinois. The personal mail from the other Kane came from Texas—Houston, I think."

Mark's mind began to race. He had just received another clue to the mystery that never really seemed to leave his thoughts since the day he first opened the dusty old manila envelope. Suddenly, Mark found himself hopeful that the daughter might know to whom her father had written the poetry. He was confident the woman to whom Kane wrote would appreciate receiving his words of love. However, Houston was a big city with a large metropolitan area. Mark would need more than simply a last name. "George, can you remember anything else?" he asked.

"Hmmm," George thought aloud. "Well, I seem to recall that the personal letters the other Kane sent were always in business envelopes." George stared off into space again, as he tried to visualize the mail he had delivered so long ago. "It was a computer company's letterhead," he finally said. "Don't remember the company name, though, but it was a computer company."

"If you can't remember the company's name," Mark asked, "how can you be so sure it was a computer company?"

"Because, I can remember the logo," George quickly replied. "They used a picture of a computer disk on their letterhead."

Mark felt as thought he had heard all George was likely to remember. "George," Mark said, as he stood and put on his coat and gloves. "You've been very, very helpful. I owe you one."

"Hell, you owe me more than one!" George countered. "You owe me so many, I've lost count. All I want to know is when can I start collecting?"

"You can collect when this record snowfall has completely melted!" Mark said, smiling back at George over his shoulder as he walked out into the brisk March morning air. With his interest in the writings of Thomas Kane sparked once again, he drove off toward his office. Mark could hardly wait to get in front of his computer and begin his search for "*someone* Kane", a computer company employee last known to live in Houston, Texas.

As she finished a morning two-mile run, Sam noticed that this year the trees were budding leaves a little sooner than was normal for the Houston area, although it could never be *too* soon for Sam. Her childhood memories of life in New England were filled with images of what she had called "stick trees"—trees without leaves. There the leaves would fall in October and would not return until May the following year. Consequently, spring never officially arrived until the new leaves came out, and of coarse summer could not start until spring was out of the way. Overall, it made for a very short spring each year.

'Let the leaves begin!' she thought to herself, as she slowed to a walk in front of her driveway. Staying fit was important to Sam and she seldom neglected her morning run. She took great pride in both her shapely figure and in her tenacious dedication to keeping it that way. Up to this point in her life, however, Sam had not harbored any deep desire to maintain a permanent relationship with anyone. Still, at twenty-nine years old, she was beginning to think differently, which made her morning exercise seem even more important.

Sam waved to her next-door neighbor, Michele, who was just beginning her own morning walk. Michele often asked Sam to join her, but Sam preferred to run. It somehow left her feeling more invigorated than when she walked. Furthermore, Sam appreciated the fact that unlike a walker, a runner didn't usually talk to anyone while exercising. To Sam's way of thinking, that was definitely a part of the positive side of running.

"Spring is almost here!" Michele called out. "Do you think it means love is in the air?"

"I'm convinced that if we are ever going to meet 'Mr. Wonderful'," Sam yelled back, "we are going to have to expand our exercise territory!" With that and a small round of laughter between them, Michele headed off down the street. Sam stooped to pick up the newspaper tossed into her driveway earlier that morning and then went inside, where she spent the next thirty minutes reading the business section of the paper while eating a light breakfast. And for Sam, breakfast routinely consisted of two pieces of toast with butter and cinnamon sugar, a multi-vitamin, and a large glass of orange juice.

Once through the paper, Sam quickly showered, then settled into the comfortable leather chair positioned in front of the oversize computer monitor on her desk. Surrounded by a litany of computer peripherals and numerous CD's, she turned on her computer.

"Good morning, Samantha," greeted the computer in a young and slightly seductive male voice. "I hope you had a restful night. Did the weather permit you to run this morning? You should know that you have six new messages in your mailbox waiting to be read."

Sam had programmed her computer with numerous voice files, replacing the standard default "beeps" and "ta-da's" wherever possible with convivial speech that appropriately changed depending upon the time of day. Moreover, Sam only allowed her computer to call her "Samantha."

"I slept fine," she replied aloud to a computer that served as a safe imitation for human companionship. "Likewise, my morning run was quite invigorating." Even though the computer could not "hear" or understand her words, Sam chose to add, "Thank you *so* much for asking."

"Now," Sam mused aloud, "let's see who has sent me mail this Monday morning." With a few rapid clicks of the mouse, the subject lines of all new e-mail messages were displayed on her screen. Sam quickly assessed the messages.

This morning's e-mail seemed typical. Three were from Paul Strickland, her supervisor at SSS - Southern Software Solutions who oversaw the application programming she did from her home in the Dallas area. One was from her friend Marcy, who was also a SSS programmer working from home. Two were unsolicited spam messages from Internet marketers. The latter never ceased to annoy Sam and she deleted the unwanted messages without opening them. She had learned the hard way that opening unwanted spam could infect a computer with viruses and she was always discriminating when it came to which e-mail to open and read and which to discard unread.

The messages from Paul included two required changes in Sam's recent programming and an update on the status of the overall project. Sam saw that she continued to be rated as "on schedule," a caveat by which she must adhere in order to be allowed to work from home. Finally, she opened the e-mail from Marcy. It read:

> Hi Sam! So, did you get lucky this weekend, or did you just sit around your house wishing you had?! Don't answer...I think I already know! Listen, Eric told me last night that an old army buddy of his is coming to Houston next weekend. I know how you hate blind dates, but I have seen this guy's picture. He is quite the hunk, if I do say so myself. So how about it? Dinner and a few decadent hours of drinking and loud music at Ruby's? It will be fun. *Please* say "yes"! Who knows, this guy might just be the one. Let me know so I can get it set up. Love 'ya! Marcy

Sam smiled. 'He *might* be the one is right,' she thought. Of course, the other side of that was that he might *not* be the one, which for the longest time had seemed to be the case. The last serious relationship in Sam's life had lasted little more than three weeks and it had been over five years ago. Since that time, she had dated a dozen or so guys, all of whom came up short in her definition of "worth the trouble and effort."

Still, Sam refused to lower her standards or change her ideas regarding romance and love, remaining true to her beliefs and dreams. She continued to look with discretion for the man with whom she would share the rest of her life. However, as she approached her thirtieth birthday, Sam was finding that the pursuit of love was becoming more painful with every romantic disappointment encountered along the way. The last thing she wanted to try right now was a blind date with a man she had never met.

Nevertheless, Marcy *was* a good friend—perhaps her best friend these days—and Sam hated to disappoint her. They had known each other now for nearly four years and had spent many hours sharing the secrets of their lives. So with an ominous feeling of dread and possible regret, Sam clicked the REPLY icon on her desktop and wrote:

Hi Marcy! No pressure, right?! You know this sort of thing really doesn't excite me, but... oh, alright. Based solely upon the fact that you are personally vouching for the fact this guy isn't a serial killer (what is his name?), I suppose it could be fun since you and Eric will both be there as well. Just remember...I do reserve the right to retreat with a proverbial headache if the situation warrants. Give me a yell with the details of when and where. I'll catch you later. Paul needs some updates made to last week's code. What are the odds of that? Love, Sam

And with a final click of the mouse, the message was gone and Sam's fate for the upcoming Saturday night was all but sealed. Still, Sam held very little hope of ever finding a nice man in this manner. She just figured that most people who resorted to blind dates were generally on the rebound from one failed relationship or another and because of that, perfect chemistry between any two on a blind date was a long shot at best. If she did have one hope, however, it was that by Sunday she would not regret accepting Marcy's insistent proposition.

'Oh well,' thought Sam, 'if nothing else, Mom will be pleased to learn that I actually went on a date, instead of sitting at home on a Saturday night curled up in bed with a romantic novel.' Upon second thought, Sam's good instincts told her not to mention anything to her mother until the day *after* the blind date. There was no good reason, she wisely thought, to get her mother all worked up before she herself knew whether the guy was worth all the maternal questions the date would engender.

With that as her final thought on the matter, Sam closed her e-mail application and began to work on the software development project that awaited her professional attention. After all, she *was* being paid to sit at home and work.

Chapter Five

he cursor on Mark's computer blinked steadily, awaiting his next command. His hope was that he was about to take his curiosity a step further by locating the daughter of Dr. Thomas Kane. Prior to this morning's conversation with George Vogel, he had not on his own learned any new information beyond what Rick Hastings had told him several months earlier.

After that conversation with Rick, Mark had immediately checked with Amy Larson, a secretary in the human resources area at Mountain View College, in an effort to learn more about Kane's daughter. At first, Amy had balked at the idea of looking through old personnel files. After all, there were federal laws protecting the privacy of the individuals who worked at the college. However, after a little coaxing and a couple of famous Benton smiles, Amy had agreed to look—but only because as she put it, "the poor man was dead and gone." Unfortunately, however, Amy could find no record of a daughter. In fact, Thomas Kane had not listed anyone as his next of kin; rather, he had provided the name of a funeral home in Horton Grove, Illinois, and had requested they be contacted in the event of his death.

Now, armed with the fast Internet connectivity offered at the college, the small amount of information gained earlier that morning at Mandy's Café and a strange yet compelling desire for answers, Mark began his search to locate Kane's daughter. If he had any chance of finding the woman Thomas Kane had loved, this seemed his last course of action. And if he could find Kane's daughter, he might also learn the identity and whereabouts of the woman to whom Kane had written his touching poetry.

Since the discovery of the old envelope, Mark had remained committed in his desire to return Kane's words to this unknown woman. He began his search by typing the word "Kane" and pressed ENTER. The Internet search engine immediately reported over 6,270,000 matches. 'Well, that won't work,' Mark thought, knowing all too well from his years of research experience that the search criteria he had entered was far too broad. Next, he typed "Thomas Kane" and pressed ENTER. This query yielded over 1,500,000 matches. He was certainly going in the right direction, but was not yet able to achieve a quick solution!

Mark decided to step back from Thomas Kane and search instead for Kane's daughter using the information George Vogel had given him. He typed "Kane Houston Texas" and marked the advanced search criteria to include "ALL OF THE WORDS", as opposed to "ANY OF THE WORDS" or "EXACT PHRASE", and pressed ENTER. This query brought back over 453,000 matches to his computer screen.

Mark knew he needed to significantly narrow down his search request if there was ever going to be a chance of locating Kane's daughter using the Internet. He once again, he decided to change his approach. He typed "hardware software Houston Texas" and pressed ENTER. This search revealed nearly 396,000 matches. Mark then typed "computer firm Houston Texas" and pressed ENTER. This slight change in one word seemed to help, as the number of matches was reduced to 322,000. Still, even this number of matches could take months to explore.

Mark took a few moments to think how else he might word his query, given the limited amount of information he had available. Up to this point, he had hesitated even trying to match the name "Kane" with a computer company. One might assume Kane's daughter was probably married and would no longer go by that last name.

Unfortunately, Mark was nearly out of options. With his confidence waning, he typed "Kane computer firm Houston Texas". He again marked the search criteria "ALL OF THE WORDS" and pressed ENTER. The computer seemed to take a little longer this time, leading Mark to believe that the number of matches would be high. After less than a second, the screen dutifully displayed the results. The search engine reported that his query yielded 22,500 matches.

"Better," Mark noted aloud, knowing he still had to get closer. Next, he typed in "Kane computer firm personnel Houston Texas." The number of matches declined once again to 4,200 matches. Then, by replacing the word "personnel" with the word "employee," his efforts were rewarded with 231 matches.

"Now that's promising," Mark said aloud, as he sent the matches to his office printer. Still, he was already thinking about all of the factors that could make the information he had just found useless. In his usual academic fashion, Mark began to write down all the mitigating factors he could imagine. After a few minutes of thought, he had written:

√ daughter married/divorced—has different last name
√ daughter no longer living
√ daughter no longer works for computer company in Houston
√ daughter no longer works in Houston for any company
√ computer company no longer in business
√ computer company not located in the city of Houston, but rather, in suburb of Houston

Mark studied the list of negating possibilities, trying to think of other logical reasons why the latest search results might not prove useful. The 231 matches to his last query now seemed somewhat less promising, given all the reasons why the links provided might not lead him to Kane's daughter. Mark tried several more Internet searches, all using different word combinations. However, none yielded any fewer results than the 231 matches he had already found.

Mark had once again reached the limit of what he knew to do, given the resources and information available to him. Certainly, there were national firms that specialized in finding missing persons. But for Mark, the search for the woman Kane loved was a diversion of fancy, rather than of necessity. He was not prepared—nor could he afford—to utilize any professional assistance in this search. Still, at least for the time being, he did have a next step. Mark had discovered 231 matches he could now begin to explore in his search for the daughter of Thomas Kane.

For the next two weeks, Mark meticulously went through each of the matches he had identified during his Internet search. By studying the matches one by one, he surmised that some could be discarded for obvious reasons. One discarded match had directed Mark to the homepage of a twelve-year old boy named Ben McCallister, a junior high school student who lived in **Kane** City, Iowa, whose interests included interactive video and **computer** games, and whose father and step-mom lived in **Houston**, **Texas**, where his father worked for an aerospace **firm**. Since all the words Mark searched for—Kane, computer, firm, Houston, and Texas—appeared on this single web page, this false lead had come back as a match.

After discarding all obvious wrong matches, Mark found himself left with 177 possibilities. His next step was to contact each of these Internet links. With his teaching responsibilities completed for the day, Mark spent the rest of this particular Friday afternoon preparing and sending e-mails to the 177 possible matches still on his list. Among those e-mail recipients were individuals whose last names were Kane and whose e-mail addresses Mark had found in the employee directories posted on the websites of computer-related, Houston-based firms. Other messages he sent directly to the human resources departments of computer-related firms based in Houston area. To all he sent the following message:

From: Mark Benton
Subject: Personal Search

Hello. My name is Mark Benton. I am a professor at Mountain View College in Preston Falls, CO. I am in possession of some private papers that belonged to Dr. Thomas Kane, a professor who passed away over three years ago. It is my hope to return these papers to Dr. Kane's next-of-kin.

> Unfortunately, the only information available to me is that he has a daughter working for a computer firm in the Houston area. If you can be of assistance in this matter, please contact me at your earliest convenience. Thank you.

Mark intentionally did not include his phone number in these e-mails. He saw no need to give his number to strangers; if they had any information, they could simply click on the REPLY icon to respond directly back to him at Mountain View College.

It was after six o'clock when Mark left his office and headed home for the weekend. With temperatures slightly below normal for this time of year, it was reassuring that the snowmelt was continuing at a pace which posed no danger for flooding to Preston Falls residents. Just yesterday, the old-timers at Mandy's Cafe had said that the slow snowmelt following their record snowfall was God-sent. As stories of floods from decades past were recounted, Mark was glad it was a phenomenon he would not have to witness.

After eating a dinner taken from the freezer to the microwave and then to the table, Mark settled into his recliner. Once again, he pulled the poems out of the envelope that had since found a new home on the end table beside the recliner in his living room. Although he had read them all many times over, he still found himself moved by the poignancy and sincerity each offered. Mark reached for the first poem on top of the stack and began to read.

"Is it that the rain makes us feel more cold and alone?
I miss you today...
I miss your smile, your smell, your warmth.
Will you grant me these things
every cold, rainy day that we are together?

I made myself hot chocolate this morning;
and, without thinking, I made enough for two.
It seems that everything I do now
I do with "us" in mind.

Being well-traveled over these many years,
I thought I knew people--
that I understood all the human emotions
God has granted in our existence.

But since I've known you,
I've come to realize, quite simply,
that is not true.

Knowing you—knowing us...
has made me question how anyone including ourselves
could ever profess to have been in love,
while not having fallen in love at first sight.

You consume my every thought now,
and every beat of my heart
is helplessly in rhythm with those thoughts.
Yet, with you ever-present in my heart and soul,
I find it increasingly difficult
to put these thoughts and feelings of love into words.

How, then, will I be able to tell you
of my undying love in all our days to come?

I can only pray that you will always
know my love from the simplest of things:
...the feeling you will get when catching my glance
from across a crowded room;
...the security you will know
from the gentle touch of my hand in yours;
...the warmth you will feel deep within
from the soft touch of my lips upon yours.

I must admit that at first,
I worried our passion would not survive
the many hours each day we spend apart.
But I now realize only those encounters
without passion succumb to absence.

Someone once wrote that the wind can
quickly extinguish the light of a small candle,
but that the same wind can also fan and fuel
the embers of a great fire meant to burn.

Absence does make a committed heart
that is forever lost in love
grow fonder.

While I do love you more today than yesterday,
you must also know
I love you less today
than I will tomorrow."

Mark set the poem aside. He could not help but think how truly powerful, yet at the same time, quietly gentle these words were. He pulled another from the stack.

"I found a message, not in a bottle,
While running along the sea.
It's just the sort of thing, you'd say,
That reminded you of me.

Growing beside the beach front path
Were violets rich in hue.
The simple beauty these flowers displayed
Reminded me of you.

I paused to capture this moment in time,
Painted in shades of blue.
The wonderful scent surrounding each one
Reminded me of you.

And while I looked, others passed;
Those who stopped were few.
No one saw the qualities that
Reminded me of you.

I knelt to touch the beauty found,
Still covered with morning dew.
The softness felt through gentle touch
Reminded me of you.

The message God had given me,
Though others may not see,
Was a blossom grown from love's abound:
The gift of you to me."

Mark set the poem aside. His mind could not help but wonder what it must be like to love someone so purely and so completely. He retrieved and read another from the stack.

"I closed my eyes and felt you.
You always stay with me long after you have gone.

Each time my mind remembers,
back comes the feel of your gentle touch...
the smell of your soft skin...
the taste of your beautiful body.

I opened my eyes, and smiled.
You excite me so.

Again, I closed my eyes and the memory continued.
I felt your warmth...
I felt your passion...
I could still see the look in your eyes:
wanting, needing... and then,
wanting more.

I remembered gazing into your eyes,
seeing looks of disbelief, ecstasy, satisfaction,
and finally, love.

I opened my eyes, and smiled.
You excite me so.

Once more I closed my eyes.
I felt your yearning embrace.
It was as though you never wanted to leave.
It was a moment when we had become one.

I opened my eyes, and smiled.
You excite me so."

Mark smiled. He felt sure Thomas Kane was writing about what it felt like to make love with... in frustration, Mark realized once again he did not know how to refer to her—the woman to whom Kane wrote these heart-felt words. Of one thing, however, Mark was sure: her identity did not lie within the writings. He had read them all many times and there was simply no reference made to her name.

The day had been long and Mark was growing tired. He pulled another sheet of paper from the stack and read the words as carefully as he had the very first time.

"Have you ever thought that certain things were just meant to be?
I miss you today...
I miss the light in your eyes, your infectious smile, and your perfume,
which lingers long after you have gone.
You truly are the love of my life.

Loving you—being loved by you...
has forever changed my life and in ways I can't explain.

You know me so well;
You read my mind instinctively,
and you know my every thought.
You never fail to cover my weaknesses with your own strengths.
You are and always have been my soul mate.

Even before we met I knew you and you knew me.
And when we met, we loved,
and we knew what we had always known.

But then came the decisions
that would affect each of our worlds;
decisions that oft times seemed too difficult to make.

I have made my decision,
and have now learned a valuable lesson of life:
The decision itself is easy;
it has already been made for us.

Decisions are easy that way because in every case,
we already know the answer.
What makes a decision seem hard, in fact,
is that we don't always like what the answer is,
or what it might mean for others.

I know we have no choice when it comes to love.
Love is a gift from God
that can neither be denied or refused.

I have made my decision.
And while it has proved to be the hardest decision
of my life
because of what it will forever mean to others,
it also has proved to be the easiest;
it really was just a matter of being honest with myself,
listening to my heart,
and realizing that I already knew the answer.

You are and always will be
the most important person in my life.

I now belong to you."

Mark reverently placed the words back inside the old manila envelope. He knew his desire to put these poems into the unknown woman's hands was growing as strong as the words themselves.

Three weeks had passed since Sam had gone on the blind date arranged by Marcy. As it turned out, the guy was not that good-looking. In fact, he was quite a bit overweight and had a somewhat annoying personality to boot. Not surprisingly, the evening had been short-lived. Marcy apologized the next morning and blamed Eric for showing her a picture of the man from ten years before.

However, Sam brought no expectations to the encounter. She chalked up the fiasco to experience and willingly forgave Marcy of any wrongdoing.

Finishing another productive day "in the office," Sam realized that on this particular day she had banged away on her computer keyboard for nearly ten hours. Working this long on a Friday was not what she intended, but Sam had no other plans. Sometimes, it was not that easy for software developers to write code—especially when the customers kept changing their minds relative to what they expected the software to accomplish within their business environments.

As she stood in the kitchen pouring herself a much deserved glass of chardonnay, Sam heard the voice of her computer. "Samantha," the computer alerted, "I hope you are having a good day. You should know you have four new messages in your mailbox waiting to be read."

Sam returned to her computer with the wine glass in hand. "Thanks," she said aloud.

She proceeded to open her e-mail and the subjects of four unread messages promptly displayed. One was from the blind date guy. He had already sent three earlier messages suggesting they get together again. Sam had deleted all three without answering. 'This guy just doesn't get it!' she thought, deleting his fourth attempt at contact without replying.

The second message was from Paul. Sam quickly decided that his could wait; her "office" was now closed until Monday morning, 8:00 AM. She tried to preserve the sanctity of her personal time by not reading work-related messages on her time off.

The third message was from Marcy. A click of the mouse brought up the message.

> Sam... Let's play tennis tomorrow at Ramsey Park. How's 10:00 AM sound? They say it's a cheap substitute for sex. love, Marcy

Sam clicked REPLY and began to type.

> Sounds good, although chocolate tastes better than sweat! See you then. love, Sam

She clicked SEND and sent her reply message on its way back to Marcy.

The fourth message listed the sender as someone named Mark Benton, with a subject line that read, "Personal Search." Sam stared at the unopened message for a moment while savoring another sip of chardonnay. Perhaps her inaction was because she knew no Mark Benton. Perhaps it was, in part, due to her fear of computer viruses that infected systems simply through the action of an unsuspecting user opening unsolicited e-mail. For whatever reason, Sam just stared at her computer screen, as she took another sip of wine.

Suddenly, she decided to give the fourth message no more thought. She moved the mouse over the subject line and promptly deleted the unread message without opening to read it.

Chapter Six

uring the week that followed, numerous e-mail replies found their way to Mark Benton's computer. Yet by Friday, Mark remained no closer in his attempt to locate Thomas Kane's daughter. The contents of those messages received were, to say the least, all over the board. Some replies from computer firms simply stated that none of their staff named "Kane" acknowledged having a father named "Thomas." Other replies indicated that management was unable to forward Mark's inquiry to its staff, since corporate policy prohibited that level of personal intrusion. One reply confirmed a company's policy of non-participation in online surveys, while another reply thanked Mark for his interest in their company and provided him with their sales brochure as an e-mail attachment.

The result of all this effort was that Mark was still unable to locate anyone named Kane working in the Houston area, whose father's name was Thomas. It had been, by anyone's estimation, a long shot at best. In an outward act of frustration, Mark hastily shut his computer down for the day. As he sat and simply stared across his office, his eyes eventually focused on a framed picture hanging on the opposite wall. It was a motivational poster commonly seen in offices, whereby management tries in a less-than-subliminal manner to encourage employees to accomplish great things. Mark had been given the poster years earlier from a retiring professor, who had been a mentor of sorts. It featured a lone rock climber hanging precariously along a vertically sheer portion of a mountain, thousands of feet from the valley floor. Under the picture in large letters was the word "PERSEVERANCE," and under that read "There is no substitute for hard work." The obvious message implied was that ultimately, to achieve any goal, one could not give up when things got tough.

'Perseverance,' Mark thought in disgust. 'It's easy to persevere when you know what your next step needs to be. Even the rock climber knows his next move—up! I'm not so sure *where* I need to turn next!' After a few moments of anguish, Mark reached for the telephone and dialed his colleague Rick.

Rick answered the call in his usual fashion, "MVC History Department; Hastings speaking."

"Rick, this is Mark."

"Hey, guy!" came Rick's up-beat reply. "What's up?"

"Do you remember a few months back," Mark began, "when I asked you about Thomas Kane, the professor who died just before we came to MVC?"

"Yeah, I remember," said Rick.

"Well," Mark continued, "I am still holding on to those personal papers found behind the file cabinet the day I moved upstairs. I have hesitated tossing them in the trash, since I am sure his daughter would appreciate getting them. My problem is I cannot seem to find her. The only thing I've been able to learn is that she probably worked for a technology firm in the Houston, Texas, area at the time of her father's death."

"How did you learn that little bit of information?" Rick asked curiously.

"How else?" quipped Mark. "I asked 'ol George Vogel if he remembered anything relative to the mail he delivered to Kane's home. Right off, he remembers that the professor received mail on a regular basis from someone, last name 'Kane,' whose letters came on some computer firm's stationery that had a return address of Houston, Texas."

Rick chuckled aloud. "Why am I not surprised? George does have the best memory in town. So let me guess. You've been using the Internet to search for his daughter and have come up dry."

"That about sums it up," confirmed Mark. "I did check with Amy over in Human Resources a while back. Interestingly, however, she could find no record of a daughter. In fact, Thomas Kane listed *no one* as his next of kin. Instead, he provided the name of a funeral home in Horton Grove, IL, and requested they be the ones contacted in the event of his death."

Rick sensed definite disappointment in Mark's voice. Both fell silent for a few seconds, before Rick suddenly asked, "Why not approach it from a different direction?"

Mark's interest perked up at the thought that his friend might be seeing something that he missed. "I would, but unfortunately I don't know what other direction to take."

"Sure you do," Rick replied. "Let's think about this. Mountain View College had no record of a daughter, yet Kane's daughter showed up a few weeks after his death to claim her father's personal things. It would seem to me that the question you have to ask yourself is, 'how did she know he died?'"

Well, there it was; the answer had been in front of him the entire time. Since the college had no instructions to contact Kane's daughter, it had to be the funeral home in Illinois that notified her of her father's death!

"Rick," Mark exclaimed with newfound purpose, "you are a genius!"

"Tell me something I don't already know," gloated Rick. "Be sure to keep me posted. I always enjoy a good mystery!"

"I sure will, pal!" Mark said and quickly ended the call. Staring once again at the computer screen in front of him, Mark immediately decided not to use the Internet. What small town funeral home would have a website anyway? Instead, he picked up the telephone again and dialed long distance information. He would speak directly to the funeral home staff. He vowed not to let them go until he had learned the name and address of Thomas Kane's daughter.

Sam had elected to stay at home alone for still another Saturday night. Going out these days was becoming more work than it was worth. On this night, Sam read a recently released romance recommended by her neighbor Michele. Finishing both the book and a good cry, she decided to pour herself a glass of wine before retiring for the evening. She wondered why she put herself through such emotional stress. The truth was she enjoyed a good romantic story and usually read every romantic novel her friends recommended.

Sam's mind wandered to thoughts of her father. She found herself remembering a class trip to Florida that her father chaperoned when she was twelve years old. As her thoughts continued to wander, she remembered the sixth grade father daughter dance. Her father had appeared self-conscious and fumbled like a young boy while trying to pin a flower corsage on her dress. At the time, she did not understood why, as his hands came close to her budding bosom, it had seemed more awkward for him than it had been for her.

Now, of course, Sam realized that it was probably because he was seeing her as a young woman for the first time and not as a little girl. She then remembered the bouquet of violets she had seen at her father's grave and with that thought, the nagging questions quickly returned.

Sam walked across the living room. Looking to the top shelf of the bookcase, she stared at the single violet placed in the tiny frame last fall. The frame sat next to a row of romance novels Sam had collected over the years. She moved some of the books aside and retrieved an old manila envelope from its hiding place behind the books. She stretched out on her couch and covered herself with an afghan her mother had made last winter. Since finding it in her father's office a few weeks after his death, Sam often looked at the contents of this envelope. She again stared intently at the outside of the envelope, hoping to discover something she had not seen or realized before now. Unfortunately, there was to be no new revelation on this particular evening.

Across the front of the envelope, she saw the words "from Amanda" written in her father's very neat and unmistakable handwriting. Sam opened the clasp and pulled out the stack of papers sheltered inside the envelope. She picked up the first sheet and read the words she now knew by heart.

"Lost and lonely, I ran through life;
Valued words seemed lies.
And when my hopes had disappeared,
You touched me with your eyes.

You reached into my heart and soul;
You chose to stay awhile.
And as I tried to understand,
You touched me with your smile.

The magic we found seemed as though
It came from up above.
And as our lives grew closer still,
You touched me with your love.

The pain I'd known passed quickly away;
You gave me rest from strife.
So simple it seemed for you to do:
You touched me with your life."

Sam set the poem aside. She took the next sheet of paper from the stack and continued to read.

"And now, too soon, we've reached the end;
Our timing seems too slow.
But take a moment to listen, my love.
There's something you should know.

You've always meant much more to me,
Than words could ever say.
Still, I never really knew how much,
Until you went away.

But most of all, I loved you more
Than any love I've known.
I loved you for the way you cared,
And the warmth that you have shown.

The memories you have left for me
Are all my dreams come true.
Yet the truest dream in my heart survives:
I'm still in love with you."

Sam pulled a tissue from a box on the end table. No matter how many times she read these words, she never failed to cry. Sometimes, her tears were for her father who she missed terribly. Sometimes, the tears resulted from the anger she felt, realizing that her father loved a woman other than her mother. And at other times, the tears were caused by the sorrow she felt for her mother, who she assumed had never known about the love that obviously existed between her father and another woman.

Sam never told her mother about finding the poetry among her father's things at the small college in Colorado. After wrestling with this issue for days, she had ultimately decided it would serve no purpose to tell her mother about the envelope, especially now that her father was gone. Her mother had been doing quite well on her own for the last fifteen years. There simply seemed no need to tell about Amanda or the poetry written to her father.

Sam continued to read the words that had come to mean so much to her.

"Sunlight shone through forest green
On wildflowers scented with dew.
Clouds slept peacefully across the sky...
I looked and I saw you.

Birds flying high sang a thousand songs,
With lyrics known only by few.
Wind-swept leaves danced merrily along...
I listened and I heard you.

A field of green, rich with life,
And soft in its radiant hew,
Lay beneath the solemn trees...
I touched and I felt you.

A bubbling stream wandered nearby,
Its pure waters vibrant and blue.
It beckoned me to its quiet banks...
I drank and I knew you.

Then suddenly the forest disappeared;
I awoke with loneliness renewed.
Still now and then, when time permits,
I remember and I miss you."

Even after looking through all of her father's personal papers last year, Sam had failed to identify this woman beyond her first name. She was unable to learn where her father had met her, or where she might be now. She could only read the words repeatedly, hoping some clue to Amanda's full identity would present itself. Sam set aside the words just read. She took another piece of paper from the stack and continued.

"I feel as though my life's complete;
I've had my dream come true:
I've found someone to know and love,
That someone being you.

Soon we'll join our lives as one;
The special magic we share
Is so unique unto this world,
It must be held with care.

For when you're away, I miss you so;
The sun above won't shine.
I try to write of the love I feel,
But the words don't seem to rhyme.

I need you now like never before,
As a lover and a friend.
Once together, I swear to you,
We will never part again."

The words grew in power and emotion each time Sam read them. Once started, she seldom stopped before reading through every one. There were twenty-eight poems in all, each describing the endearing love a woman named Amanda felt for Sam's father. If Sam had simply picked up a book of poetry and had read these words, she might not have been as moved. These, however, were the words of a woman Sam had never met, but who had loved Sam's father in ways that she never felt with any of the men in her life. Sam wiped away her tears and read another.

"Our love has grown so deep and true;
We've made our future plans.
But the love we've nurtured for so long
Is slipping through our hands.

So sad was the day you went away;
I stood and watched you go.
The pain of living our lives apart
Has forced my love to grow.

For although you've gone, the love remains;
It grew from your first touch.
And from that moment shared with me,
I've loved you, oh, so much.

Because of this love, I swear to you,
When we're together again,
I'll spend each day showing you why
It will never, ever end."

Sam could tell from the collective words of the twenty-eight poems that Amanda and Sam's father had met, had fallen in love, and in the end had gone their separate ways. What she did not know was why they were unable to stay together. It was obvious that Amanda had still loved him, even after they had parted. Sam suspected that perhaps her father fell out of love with Amanda. After all, he *had* fallen out of love with her mother. 'Perhaps,' Sam thought, 'this was a definite pattern of behavior.'

With both her wine glass and the box of tissues now empty, Sam decided to read one more of Amanda's poems before retiring for the evening. She reached for the next one in the stack.

"The leaves are falling; the green is gone;
A chill has filled the air.
Alone, I paused to shed a tear,
And remember when you were there.

So rich the wealth you gave to me:
Your warmth, your love, your smile.
For all my life, I'll never regret
You chose to stay awhile.

So short our time together seemed,
Forever memories I'll hold.
Each time we kissed, the magic spoke
A thousand words untold.

And now you're gone; I miss you so.
I know I always will.
But most of all, when I think of you,
I know I love you still."

Where was Amanda now? Why didn't the love between Amanda and her father survive? Would Sam like her if she knew her? Did she even want to know this woman? These were only a few of the questions haunting the memory of the daughter of a very private man.

Sam fell asleep on the couch that night. Instead of dreaming of the father she did not know, Sam dreamed of the one she did… of a dad she would always love.

Chapter Seven

hat city, please?" said a voice completely lacking intonation or emotion. It might as well have been a computer, Mark thought. For all he knew, it could be just that.

"Horton Grove, Illinois," Mark replied.

"What listing?" the voice asked dryly.

"I need the number for the local funeral home in Horton Grove," Mark said, "but I'm afraid I don't know the name." Amy in the personnel office had not mentioned the name of the funeral home to Mark when she had looked for Kane's next-of-kin. Therefore, calling information was another shot in the dark. For all Mark knew, there was no funeral home in Horton Grove, which would mean he would have to start searching the surrounding communities to find the funeral home responsible for Kane's burial.

The response was immediate. "I show one listing for funeral services—a Bernard Funeral Home," came the reply. "The number is area code 618-772-2844. Shall I connect you?"

Mark jotted down the number, knowing he was getting close now. "Yes, please," he replied. The operator made the connection without saying another word.

On the third ring, and much to his dismay, Mark heard a pre-recorded message stating that the office hours were from 8:00 AM to 5:00 PM, Monday through Friday. The recording also gave a number for after-hours service, implying that, if one was in the need of an undertaker on Saturday or Sunday, one was available. Mark suddenly realized there was a one-hour time difference between Illinois and Colorado.

Reluctantly, Mark put the receiver down. He sensed it was going to be a very long weekend.

After a Monday full of software debugging, Sam found herself both frustrated and mentally exhausted. Having enough for one day, she exited from her programming applications, closed her e-mail utility, shutdown the computer's operating system, and turned off the power to her laptop computer. Sam preferred a laptop computer to the bulkier desktop units, since it allowed her to work from virtually anywhere. She had never been one who allowed herself to be chained at a desk, nor did she possess a "work cubicle" mentality. While Sam did have a horrendous work ethic, she also demanded as much freedom as she could get. Working from home with her laptop computer provided an environment with the personal latitude she sought.

At the same time Samantha Kane ended her workday, Mark Benton finished teaching his last class of the day. By Mark's calculations, early afternoon in Colorado meant it was still before 5:00 PM in the Midwest. He returned to his office, closed the door, and quickly sat down at his desk. After retrieving a crumpled piece of paper from his shirt pocket, he dialed the number for Bernard Funeral Home in Horton Grove, Illinois.

After four rings, his wait was rewarded by a voice that spoke with a slow, yet distinctive, Midwestern accent. "Hello, Bernard's Funeral Home. How can we be of assistance this afternoon?"

Upon politely introducing himself, Mark learned he was speaking to Samuel Bernard, son of William Bernard, founder of Bernard Funeral Home. Mark proceeded to explain the reason for his call. "I am calling from Mountain View College, in Preston Falls, Colorado. Recently, I found some personal letters in my office that belonged to the previous occupant, a Dr. Thomas Kane. However, returning the items is proving difficult. You see, Dr. Kane passed away in October of 1996. The only information I have been able to find thus far is that you provided the services for his funeral and burial. Can you please check your records and tell me if this was the case? And if so, would you have a record of a next-of-kin I might notify regarding the personal letters I found?"

"No need to check any records," Samuel Bernard replied without hesitation. "I have lived in Horton Grove all my life and have served this community for the last thirty-one years. I remember every person who passes—where they lived, who their parents were, and, in most cases, what became of their children."

"Yes, sir, I'm sure you do," Mark said approvingly and with measured patience. He was convinced he was getting close to learning new information. Still, he did not want to place unnecessary or unwelcome pressure inadvertently on the man on the phone. "What can you tell me about Thomas Kane?"

"Well, Thomas Kane grew up right here in Horton Grove, as did his parents," Samuel began. "As I recall, Thomas joined the Marines right out of high school—wanted to serve his country during the Vietnam War. As fate would have it, however, he never did see any action—spent his entire tour of duty stuck behind a desk stateside. Nevertheless, his parents—Bill and Susan Kane—were still just as proud of him as they could be. I suppose *relieved* might be more like it, seeing that their only child was never put into harm's way. You know, many of our boys never made it back from over there. What did you say your name was again?"

"Mark Benton, sir, calling from Preston Falls, Colorado," Mark politely replied.

"Benton," echoed Samuel thoughtfully. It was almost as though the funeral director was searching his memory to see if there might have been a Benton relative right there in Horton Grove's history.

"Right…well, anyway, Thomas returned to Horton Grove after his hitch in the service was up. He worked a few odd jobs around the county, before finally deciding to go off to college—University of Illinois as I remember—to take advantage of the G.I. Bill. Did you know they are thinking of doing away with the G.I. Bill? These young boys today will have to put away their own money for college. Makes you wonder what's in it for a young fellow these days."

"No, sir, I did not know that," Mark replied. He was finding it extremely hard not ask about Kane's daughter. "I guess the blessing for us today is that young men and women are still willing to serve."

"Well, I suppose," replied Samuel Bernard in a tone that seemed less than convinced. "Anyway, it seems that college suited Thomas, because he never really quit once he started—first one degree, then another, and then another. Fortunately, Bill and Pauline got to see him become a doctor before each of them passed. I can tell you, they sure were proud of that boy. Even when his marriage ended in divorce, they still thought he could do no wrong. And they were just as proud of that daughter of his, too."

"A daughter?" Mark asked. 'Here it comes!' he thought, barely able to contain the overwhelming anticipation rising within him.

"Well, *sure*! They were just as proud of his daughter," continued Mr. Bernard, in a somewhat challenging tone. "Why wouldn't they be?"

"I'm sure they were proud," Mark quickly offered. "I just didn't realize there was a daughter." Mark instantly felt a tinge of guilt for speaking less than the truth.

"Yes, Thomas had a daughter," said Mr. Bernard. "You know, except as a very small child, I don't know I ever saw the daughter here much before Thomas' funeral. I remember they did come back occasionally to visit, as kids that move away from their parents will do—mostly on holidays—but, Bill and Pauline both passed within two years of each other, back when Thomas' daughter was still very young. I do not believe I ever saw Thomas or his family after that. I think they all lived out East somewhere. I did know that Thomas had ended up in Colorado after his divorce, because of the arrangements he made with us a few years later. He asked that in the event of his death he be returned here to Horton Grove, to be buried next to his parents. As I recall, not many turned out for his funeral, though, what with him having been gone for so many years and all."

Mark's impatience was becoming hard to contain. "Did his daughter attend the funeral?" he asked. Immediately, he realized how stupid the question must have sounded.

"Well, of course she did!" Mr. Bernard said in obvious disbelief that the question had even asked. "I called her myself, as mandated by the instructions Thomas left with us. For nearly 75 years now, we at Bernard Funeral Home have prided ourselves with a family tradition of reliable and impeccable service to our customers. We carry out each individual's final wishes as though they were our very own wishes."

"I am sure the members of your community depend upon your diligence during such times," Mark replied, then quickly pressed on. "Mr. Bernard, as I mentioned earlier, I found some personal items in my office that belonged to Thomas Kane. If you might recall the daughter's name and a telephone number where she might be reached, I can notify her regarding these personal items and forward them on to her."

"Well," Samuel said thoughtfully, "let's take a look here at my file cards—never saw the need for a computer, you understand. These cards have served my family well, since our business began."

'Yes, I know,' thought Mark, 'they've served the community for nearly 75 years now. Let's just hope they serve us now!'

After a few agonizingly long moments, broken only by the occasional self-mutterings of Samuel Bernard, the son of William Bernard, founder of Bernard Funeral Home, the wait finally ended. And just as quickly, so ended Mark Benton's search.

"Samantha Kane. 343 Cedar Pointe—and that's 'Pointe' *with* a final 'e'—Houston, TX, 77299. The telephone number I have is 921-375-7118."

That was it. There was nothing more Mark needed. He had finally uncovered the name and whereabouts of Thomas Kane's daughter, assuming of course she still lived at that address. Mark politely thanked Samuel Bernard and hung up the telephone. He stared at the information just discovered. Samantha Kane. Well, there it was. With his mind racing, he reached again for the phone. The moment had finally arrived.

As Sam walked to the kitchen for a glass of Southern-style iced tea—the kind that has an alarming amount of real sugar added—the telephone rang. Her immediate reaction was to not answer it and allow it to ring. It was probably Paul, with some last minute correction to the files she had transmitted earlier.

The telephone dutifully rang a second time. 'Well, if not corrections,' Sam thought, 'then a new assignment that would be "critically important".' Her workday was officially over, so Sam continued to let the phone ring.

Persistent in its mission, the telephone rang a third time. Sam now began to argue with herself. 'I suppose it might be Mom calling,' she thought and reluctantly walked over to the phone.

As the telephone rang for a fourth time, Sam picked up the receiver before her answering machine took the call.

"Hello," she said flatly.

"Hello," came the stumbling reply of a young male voice. It was almost as though the caller had been caught off guard. "I am calling for Samantha Kane."

"Speaking," Sam offered flatly, already weary that still another telemarketer had gained access to her unpublished telephone number.

The young, yet deep, masculine voice continued. "Hi. My name is Mark Benton. I am a professor at Mountain View College in Preston Falls, Colorado. Before I bother you needlessly, may I ask if your father happened to teach here at Mountain View College a few years ago? If not, then I apologize for bothering you this afternoon."

Sam's reaction was immediate but measured. "Yes, my father taught there. Dr. Thomas Kane. Did you know him?"

"Yes... ah, I mean, no..." The fact that he made his living as a professor of the English language suddenly failed Mark. He realized that for all his planning, he had never thought about *how* he would tell Thomas Kane's daughter about her father's poetry. What had always felt like the right thing to do was now proving extremely difficult to explain.

"What I mean to say," Mark continued, "is that I know *of* your father, but I never actually met him. I grew up in Preston Falls, went away to college, and have only been back home teaching at Mountain View College for a little over three years now."

"Well, Mr. Benton, you must have arrived at Mountain View shortly after my father passed away," Sam concluded.

"Please, call me Mark, and, yes," he replied, "it was a few weeks later. When I arrived, the office I was assigned was Room 038 in the basement of Riggins Hall."

"Riggins Hall, Room 038," Sam repeated. "Wasn't that my father's office?"

"Your memory serves you well," complimented Mark. "It was your father's office. Anyway, I used that office for nearly three years. A few months ago, however, I was reassigned to an office space on the second floor of Riggins Hall, so your father's old office is once again empty."

Sam began to wonder if Mark Benton was ever going to get to the point. Reminiscing about a place she knew nearly nothing about held very little promise.

"So, Mark," she said, taking him up on his offer to use his first name, "how can I help you?"

"Well, Samantha," Mark replied, finding himself once again measuring words very carefully. "It is because I recently moved out of your father's old office that I have been trying to find you."

Sam suddenly realized she liked the way Mark pronounced her full name. "I'm quite sure I have no clue what you are talking about," she answered.

"I'm sorry. I know I must not be making a lot of sense," Mark said apologetically and quickly continued. "You see, when I moved out of the basement of Riggins Hall, I took all of my furniture with me, since the new office space lacked furniture. Anyway, when we moved the furniture from your father's old office, an envelope was discovered behind one of the filing cabinets."

"An envelope?" repeated Sam. Her mind immediately began to wonder if perhaps it was more poetry written by Amanda. Sam tried to hide this sudden rise in interest and asked, "What kind of envelope?"

"It was a large manila envelope," replied Mark. "At first, I thought it might be one of my own envelopes, filled with student essays or exams. Actually, I didn't even look inside the envelope right away. I continued with the move and it wasn't until the end f the day that I took a second look at it. There was nothing written on the outside, so I opened the envelope and looked inside. It was then I quickly realized that the envelope was not mine."

"Are you saying that it was my father's?" Sam asked in an even voice. It seemed the mystery of her father's life was about to open still another chapter.

"I can only assume that to be the case," said Mark. "The envelope contains papers of a personal nature—documents I thought someone might want returned. However, none of the papers have any specific names on them, so I am only guessing that they belonged to your father."

Sam was almost afraid to ask. "What kind of papers are they? I mean, are they business letters, academic papers, or what exactly?"

"Well," Mark stammered, "they are, well…love poems."

'Could it be?!' Sam thought. 'Are these more poems from Amanda?' Suddenly out of nowhere, here was a chance for her to learn more about the most private side of her father's life. Sam never understood exactly why her father kept his relationship with Amanda a secret from her. More and more, she was determined to find out why.

Suddenly feeling as though Mark's unexpected phone call was an epiphany of sorts, Sam was now more interested than ever before to find this woman, and to learn what role she played in her father's life. She also wanted to know if this woman had anything to do with her parent's divorce.

"Samantha, are you still there?" Mark asked, concerned that he had said something wrong.

"Yes," Sam quickly answered. "I guess I'm just not sure what to say."

"Well," continued Mark, "I can tell you that these poems are the most poignant, endearing poetry I have ever read. And as an English professor, I certainly have read a lot!"

"Really?" replied Sam somewhat aloof, yet knowing all too well how beautiful Amanda's words could sound.

"Absolutely," Mark confirmed. "It is beautiful poetry. I knew immediately when I found the poems they should be returned. Words easily become lost in our lives and when you have an opportunity to preserve them you *must* make every effort to do so. When I asked my colleagues who used the office before me, I learned it was your father. Then, others at MVC told me that you were seen packing your father's things a few weeks after his death."

With the conversation going better than expected, Mark now hoped to learn the identity of the woman in Thomas Kane's poetry. He already knew that Samantha was Thomas' daughter from an early marriage. Still, he wanted to be careful not to offend Kane's daughter in any way by asking the wrong kinds of questions.

"Since I was unable to locate your mother," continued Mark, "you became my only hope of getting this collection of romantic poems returned to her."

Sam quickly decided that although she was beginning to enjoy talking with this man, she would keep her knowledge of Amanda to herself. She still was not completely sure if this Mark Benton had any motive beyond that already stated.

"Yes," Sam said, "a few weeks did pass after my father's death before I made the trip to Preston Falls. I was just not up to it right away. And my mother gets older, I'm afraid she doesn't care much for traveling."

"I understand completely," offered Mark. "I lost both of my parents several years ago and I know how difficult it can be to take care of these things."

"I'm sorry to hear that," Sam responded with automatic respect. "So, Mr. Benton—I mean, Mark—how many poems are there in this envelope you found?"

"Well," replied Mark, "if memory serves me, there are ninety-two in all—some short and some long. Yet, each and every one of them portrays an endearing testament of the love shared by your mother and father."

Mark continued in his surreptitious effort to get Sam to divulge that her mother and father had been divorced for some time and that her father had written this poetry to a woman other than her mother. He continued to hope that somewhere in all of this was a story. With Thomas Kane now gone, Mark really wanted to find this woman and learn more about this story of unrequited love.

Sam, on the other hand, assumed that Amanda had written the poems to her father and did not feel the need to elaborate on this fact to a complete stranger. Besides, since she knew nothing about Amanda, there was not much to tell even if she had felt like sharing.

"Samantha," said Mark, "I want you to know that the words have had a significant impact on me." Mark knew he had to push the issue if he ever had any hope of uncovering the complete story.

"As a matter of fact," he continued, "I was hoping to write a story surrounding this romantic bond between two people deeply in love. Is it possible that I could interview your mother at a later point, after she has an opportunity to reunite herself with this poetry?"

"I will have to get back to you on that," Sam quickly responded in a succinct, yet elusive manner. "Mark, I am grateful that you took the time to find me. Would it be a problem for you to mail the envelope down to me?"

"Not at all," Mark assured her. And even though Samuel Bernard had provided her address to him, he dutifully said, "Just give me your mailing address and I'll drop it in the mail tomorrow."

Sam first considered giving Mark the address of her post office box, where all of her business mail was delivered. After all, she really did not know this person and it was always better to err on the side of caution. She quickly decided against it, however, since it would require a trip to the post office every day to check for the envelope's arrival. Instead, she decided to give him her street address.

"Just send the envelope," instructed Sam, "to 343 Cedar Pointe, Houston, TX, 77299. Again, I want to thank you, Mark, for calling and for your willingness to return the envelope to me."

Sensing that Sam was not going to say anything Mark wanted to hear, he bid her farewell.

"You're quite welcome," he said. "And, listen, I will put my address and phone number in the envelope, just in case you need to contact me. It was nice talking with you, Samantha. Goodbye."

"It was nice talking to you, too, Mark," Sam responded. "Goodbye."

For Sam, the call had been quite unexpected. She found herself quite anxious to read more of the poems Amanda had written to her father. Even though Mark Benton said no names mentioned in the poetry, Sam hoped she might discern some clue to Amanda's whereabouts that Mark could not. It seemed at the very least to be a bit of good fortune, further fueling her desire to learn more about the woman her father loved.

For Mark on the other hand, the call had been disappointing. He had hoped to learn the identity of Thomas Kane's lover. Instead, he had once again come up empty.

'Oh well,' Mark thought after he hung up the phone. 'At least, I can get this material into the hands of Thomas Kane's daughter.'

Mark had hesitated revealing his knowledge of Kane's divorce on the outside chance that Samantha Kane was unaware of the other love in her father's life. Given the way the phone call had gone, Mark now thought he was probably right to do so.

As he left the Mountain View College campus that day, Mark resolved to never again try to solve any great mystery in life—especially any mystery rich in romance. Clearly, romance was not to be his strong suit in life.

Furthermore, it appeared as though Mark's 'great American novel' was going to have to wait. As he drove past Mandy's Restaurant on his way home, Mark found himself grateful he had elected *not* to share his hopes for a story with his older friends. Fact was, Mark Benton was not so sure anymore there was even a story here worth telling.

Chapter Eight

he week following Mark Benton's telephone call seemed like an eternity to Sam. Every afternoon at 2:00 PM, she dutifully watched the mailbox at the end of her driveway for the mail to be delivered. However, her watchful vigilance thus far had yielded only junk mail and an occasional bill.

On Thursday, her neighbor Michele commented she must be looking for something very important, given the way she was quickly retrieving her mail each day. Michele knew that Sam was apt to let her mail accumulate for several days at a time.

"Yes, I suppose I am" was all that Sam felt obliged to say, as she waved to Michele in cordial response.

Sam found herself obsessed with thoughts of what she might learn about Amanda from the newfound poems. More importantly, she could perhaps learn clues to Amanda's current whereabouts. In this, the second envelope to find its way to her, Sam hoped to find some hidden or ambiguous reference to a thing or place which might provide her the clue she had been looking to find.

Sam had decided while waiting for Mark Benton's package to arrive that she did in fact want to contact Amanda. This decision now gave her a sense of purpose never before felt. Today, she reconfirmed that decision as she walked back from the mailbox empty-handed yet again.

Later that same evening, Sam decided to again read the poetry already in her possession. Although she had read them many times, Sam wanted to discern which poems if any would be more meaningful this particular evening. It seemed that every time she read the words, a different passage would stick with her during the days that followed.

Sam moved the books on the top shelf of her bookcase—books used to hide the old manila envelope from the prying eyes of her mother—and reached for the crumpled package. She sat on her couch and covered herself in usual fashion with her favorite afghan. Not knowing which poem her fingers would grasp first, she pulled a sheet of paper from the envelope.

"Alone at night I wonder
If you ever remember the days,
When we were one together
In so many special ways.

Remember the tender love we shared,
Knowing it would last?
Remember the plans for marriage we made,
In our days of future passed?

Remember the times we laughed together,
Standing side by side?
Remember the very first fight we had,
When I ran away and cried?

Remember the first kiss we secretly shared,
And knew it was meant to be?
Remember those heartbreaking words you spoke
On your last day with me?

Remember all of the joys we felt?
I know I always will.
But most of all, for I can't forget,
I know I love you still."

Sam set the poem aside. She found herself wondering what parting words her father had spoken to Amanda that day. Sam continued to be unsure of exactly who left whom, since she had thus far been unable to piece together the exact details of this haunting love story. Whatever those last words might have been, they were, by Amanda's explication, *heartbreaking*. Sam pulled another sheet of paper from the envelope.

"I fear the end is drawing near;
Our special magic seems gone.
I desperately try to understand
What suddenly went wrong.

Indeed we were two lonely halves,
When united became whole.
Yet for all our efforts to coincide,
Our timing seemed too slow.

It now appears there's not much hope;
Allow me time to mourn.
I've given all my love to you...
My heart is tired and worn.

So like the teary dime-store books
That are bought and read each day,
Turn the last page in our story of love,
And I'll quickly fade away.

Yes, the end is sadder than I had thought;
I'm sorry I wasted your time.
Just remember our love on lonely nights
As a poem that could not rhyme."

'Could not or *would* not,' thought Sam, as she began to think of the possibilities. She read the poem again, but was unable to decide. Was it their love that failed to sustain the two of them, or did the two of them fail to sustain their love?

Sam suddenly felt the need for a glass of chardonnay. Setting the poem aside, she headed to the kitchen. Sam poured the wine then returned to the comfort of her couch, the warmth of her afghan, and the solace afforded by Amanda's poetry. Pulling another from the old envelope, she carefully read the romantic prose.

"I turned the music way down low,
But still the song came through.
My mind rehearsed a thousandth time
The memory of you.

My heart beat rhythmically to the notes,
Each lyric of melody.
It reminded me of so long ago,
A love that used to be.

I closed my eyes and tried to forget;
It was all that I could do.
But the feeling remained, and still I knew
The beauty of loving you.

I guess the pain will never pass;
I'll carry it for all time.
Each song I hear will bring regret:
No longer are you mine."

Sam liked this particular poem. As a woman who had both loved and who had lost at love, she identified with Amanda's apparent propensity to drown her romantic sorrows in music. The problem with using music to forget, however, was that by its very nature, it made you remember. Sam felt certain this was what Amanda was trying to say and agreed wholeheartedly with the emotion conveyed in these words.

Sam placed the poem aside, pausing to sip her wine. 'A good wine is like a woman,' her mother had told her once. 'The more it ages, the more full-bodied it becomes'—or something to that effect. Sam smiled to herself and pulled another sheet of paper from the envelope.

> "I have mine, as you have yours;
> Perfect, or so it seems.
> But when I need what he can't give,
> I have you in my dreams.
>
> At home or work, near or far -
> It doesn't matter where;
> I close my eyes and think of you,
> And magically you are there.
>
> You listen when I need to talk;
> You talk when I need to hear.
> You're my friend no matter what my mood -
> A friendship I hold dear.
>
> For in my dreams the world can't know
> The special place we play.
> No one else can feel your touch,
> Or hear the words you say.
>
> We laugh as we walk along our way
> Through fields of violets blue.
> I stop and tenderly kiss your lips
> To make my dream come true.

But suddenly I awake for the thousandth time,
And know the dream's not real.
Still I smile for having been blessed to know
The way you make me feel."

Sam stared at the poem, as though seeing it for the first time.

"Well, I'll be…!" Sam said aloud, her voice trailing off in explosive thought. How could she have missed this?! Even though she had read it many times, she never before made this connection. Yet, there it was—right on the paper in front of her—something she had missed.

"…we laugh as we walk along our way
through fields of *violets* blue…"

Sam's eyes immediately shot to the top shelf of her bookcase. There, staring right back at her was the single violet she had placed in the tiny frame last fall. With her heart beginning to race, she went to the shelf and picked up the small frame.

The violet, perfect in its form, was still as beautiful as it was the day she pulled it from among the other violets lying atop her father's gravestone. The flower had retained its deep blue color over the months, successfully maintaining its original look. Sam now saw this simple flower of nature in a way never before seen. Suddenly, it became a legitimate possibility that Amanda was the one who placed the flowers at her father's gravesite last October!

Sam brought the flower back to the couch. Setting the small frame on the table beside her, she pulled another poem from the old envelope. As fate would have it, the poem Sam now held was another one of her favorites.

"Deep within the forest green
A lone bird came to rest.
Many were the miles it came
To nurture another nest.

And while it watched upon that bough
For a match to come its way,
Voices heard from the path below
Confirmed its need to stay.

Soon the voices turned to shapes
Of two, hand in hand.
They spoke of weather and simple things,
Amidst the beauty of land.

They stopped and gazed in each other's eyes
Beneath the silent bird.
And with that look spoke a thousand words
That only Nature heard.

For a different path had brought them both
Together to stand as one.
And the watching bird knew from high
A cycle of life had begun.

The couple knew their lives just changed;
To her smile he gave a nod.
And the bird gave flight as love was born,
Made by the hand of God."

After months of reading these words and often with mixed emotions, Sam now found herself no longer disliking Amanda on any level. She finally accepted the fact that Amanda had loved her father in a way most could only hope and dream. How fortunate any man would be—especially her own father—to know a woman's love as deep and pure as the love Sam saw in these poems.

Sam dreamed that night, but her dreams were not of her father or Amanda. Instead, Sam dreamed this particular night of a man she loved—a man, however, whose face was not recognizable to her. In her dreams, this man had come to her from another world, someplace other than her own. And when this man came into her life, she instantly knew she had found her soul mate. Together, Sam and her newfound love walked down the many paths Amanda had described in her poems—through forests and meadows, along brooks and streams. And in her dream, the two even stopped to pick violets they found growing along the way.

Friday morning, Sam recalled nearly every detail of her dream. However, she could not recall the man's face. Nor could she remember where the two of them were going on their journey. But for Sam, her most overwhelming memory of the dream was the love felt between the two of them.

'So now I'm dreaming about all this! These poems are really starting to get to me!' Sam thought in quiet exasperation, as she put the breakfast dishes into the dishwasher. Intent on shifting her focus from Amanda's poetry, Sam threw herself into the latest programming challenge awaiting her attention. Given it was Friday, she really needed to wrap up her current project. Paul Strickland had e-mailed Sam earlier in the week, informing her that two new projects were waiting in the wings.

'It never stops!' she thought, as she turned on her laptop computer and began to work.

Signs of spring could be seen all around Preston Falls. As Mark entered Mandy's Café on this, the sunniest morning in the last four days, he noticed that the flowers Jenny had planted last year in the flower boxes outside the restaurant entrance had overnight suddenly sprung into full bloom. The brightly colored petals of the daisies and tulips were strategically surrounded by grass-like sweet woodruff, making the arrangement an attractive addition to the front of Mandy's Café.

"Morning, Mark," Jenny said from behind the counter. "Breakfast?" she asked. Mark could see that Martin Dobbs, Bob Tyler, and George Vogel were camped at their usual table.

"Hi, Jen," replied Mark, as he made his way to the back table. "I'll just take a cup of coffee today, please."

"Well, where has your appetite gone this morning?" Bob immediately wanted to know. However, before Mark could get a word out in response, Martin started in on him as well.

"He's probably in love!" Martin quickly said, with a laugh.

"Well, that certainly explains why you're so damn fat!" George threw back into Martin's face. "No one ever loved your sorry ass!"

And with that, as fast as it had come, the sword of ridicule was pulled from one and thrust into another. Bob Tyler laughed so hard he nearly spilled his coffee. Martin's face was as red as the stripes in the plaid tablecloth. Moreover, George, forever the instigator of such derision, was as comfortable and content as a Cheshire cat with a mouse, basking in the knowledge that his work, at least for the moment, was done.

"Marty," Mark asked in a consoling, understanding manner, "when are you ever going to learn?"

"Damn you, George," Martin responded, ignoring Mark altogether. "I've had more women in my time than you ever dreamed of having. Why, I remember one time while on ship's leave in the Philippines, I shacked up for six days with the prettiest little mama-san you can imagine, and we..."

"Whoa, boys!" Jenny interjected firmly, as she re-filled everyone's coffee cup. "I'm sure I speak for everyone in the café this morning when I say you are sharing just a little too much information."

"Yeah, Marty," yelled Stan Frazier from across the café. Stan, a local insurance agent not indigenous to Preston Falls, seldom got involved in these blue-color conversations, trying instead to appear the ever-professional businessman. "Some of us are trying to eat!"

"Oh, who asked you anyway?" Martin grumbled in obvious defeat.

"If you must know," Mark said, "I'm simply not hungry. Besides, I've only got a few minutes this morning, so coffee will just have to do."

George was unable to discern what was on Mark's mind these days, but he could tell something was consuming the young professor's thoughts. Over the past couple of months, Mark had grown a bit distant relative to his outgoing nature, now beginning to speak less and listen more. George knew that for a young person like Mark, it meant his thoughts were elsewhere.

"Is there anything going on you'd like to share, son?" he asked Mark with parental-like curiosity and concern.

"Nothing comes to mind," Mark replied, as he hurriedly drank his coffee without waiting for it to cool. He could already tell this was going to be one of those occasions where the least amount of time spent at this breakfast table, the better. "I have been doing a lot of reading lately, and, well, I suppose I just need to get out in the sun for awhile."

"The weatherman over at WNRC is calling for a real nice weekend," Bob reported.

"That sounds great," said Mark. "I think I'll try to get in some tennis tomorrow." He finished his coffee and rose to his feet. "Gentlemen," he said, as he laid a dollar on the table for Jenny, "always a pleasure."

"You're not fooling me," George said evenly as Mark was leaving. "You're going to tell me sooner or later what's been going on in that head of yours." Mark only answered with a famous Benton smile and headed out the door of the café.

As he drove the terminally dirty Jimmy toward Mountain View College, Mark's thoughts returned to the telephone call he had shared on Monday with Samantha Kane. He felt certain that by now she had received the package he had sent immediately following their conversation.

As he pulled into a parking space outside Riggins Hall, Mark realized his current and somewhat distant mood was probably the result of disappointment in not having heard anything back from Samantha. Even though she had made no promise to contact him again, Mark still found himself hoping he would be able to discuss the story with her at some point. But upon asking himself if it was the story or if it wad something else he was hoping to accomplish, Mark quickly dismissed all thoughts of Samantha Kane and began to think about the 19th century literature lecture he was giving at 10:00 AM that morning.

Sam stretched in her chair, glanced at the clock on the wall, and saw it was nearly three o'clock. She had skipped her lunch, but her current project was finally complete. She saved a copy of the project files on her hard drive and e-mailed a copy of the work to Paul. Finally, she headed for the kitchen to satisfy that most basic of human needs—hunger.

"Tuna salad on rye sounds good," she said aloud. Moments later, Sam sat at the small kitchen table, enjoying her late lunch. Since Marcy was still on spring vacation, Sam found herself wondering what she would do later that evening. For the moment, she was without her best friend, who was lying somewhere on a beach near Destin, Florida, soaking up as much sun and fun as possible.

Suddenly, Sam realized it was past the time when her mail usually came. She immediately headed outside, chewing the last bite of tuna salad while walking down the driveway. As she approached the mailbox, she could see that there was a large white envelope rolled up and stuffed inside in such a manner that the mailbox door stayed open.

"Yes!" she exclaimed aloud, as she pulled out the envelope, closed the mailbox door, and headed back inside. Mark Benton's package had finally arrived!

Sam felt a sudden excitement. She believed she was about to read more poetry Amanda had written to her father, writings that might very well provide answers to Sam's many questions. Sam went directly to the couch and settled in for some much-anticipated reading. As she reached for her afghan, Sam thought to herself, 'This is not going to be such a boring Friday evening after all!'

Chapter Nine

ark's handwriting was bold and distinct. He had not asked if Sam was married, and Sam had not offered the information. Mark had no alternative but to address the package to "Ms. Samantha Kane." As Sam stared at the handwritten address label, she realized she never really cared for "Ms.", as it somehow seemed a reminder to her and an announcement to others that she was still a single woman whose clock was ticking louder each day. And with each year that passed, her mother served that purpose with relentless devotion, "Ms." notwithstanding.

'On the other hand,' she now thought, 'I suppose I'd be offended if he had used "Miss" in an assumption I was single!' With that thought and an undeniable anticipation building within her, Sam opened the over-sized mailing envelope. Her hands trembled slightly as she reached inside, only to find yet another envelope. With a deliberate and almost reverent motion, she pulled out what appeared to be an older manila envelope of the same type and color as the one already in her possession.

Sam stared at the manila envelope she now held in her hands. Her thoughts wandered, as she again tried to imagine who Amanda was and where she might be today. Mark had mentioned on the phone that there might very well be a story in all of this. And for the first time, Sam thought he just might be right. Certainly, the poetry Amanda wrote to her father was deeply personal. That was probably why it had such appeal to Sam—the fact that it was so real gave it a meaning that easily touched the heart of the reader.

Flipping the envelope from one side to the other, Sam studied both sides. Unlike the one found among her father's personal effects three years before, there was no writing on the outside of this old manila envelope. It did, however, seem to be holding much more paper than the other envelope hidden high on her bookcase.

Sam's fingers found the clasp on the back. She pulled up the small metal wings and opened the envelope flap. Reaching inside, Sam took hold of all the papers at once and gently began removing them from the place where they had remained until recently hidden for the past several years. As her eyes watched what was being pulled from the old manila envelope, Sam suddenly found herself desperately trying to catch her breath. She had not prepared herself for what she was seeing.

Sam's hands began to tremble slightly, in the same way they had at her father's funeral. She recalled thinking then it was a visible reaction she could not control. In fact, she worried it may be a weakness and hoped others would not notice. Now, sitting alone in her living room, the "weakness" had returned.

What was before her now was both evident and unmistakable. These papers were handwritten, whereas the contents of the other manila envelope were printed. Still, this fact alone was not what sent a chill throughout Sam's body. Rather, it was the fact that Sam was looking at her father's handwriting.

After the last student on his calendar for the week thanked him for clarifying the examples of iambic pentameter presented in class earlier that day, Mark left with the same sense of urgency shared by all college students on Friday afternoons. These days, it was not often when Mark felt the youthful excitement of knowing that classes for the week were over. At this point in his life, the end of the workweek seemed more of an anticlimax, rather than a prelude to a weekend of fun and games.

Mark gathered up the homework assignments turned in by students earlier that day. Along with some reading material he had selected from the campus library, he placed the papers into his briefcase. Turning off his office light, he closed the door and headed for the parking lot.

'Optional Friday,' Mark thought to himself, in reference to the fact that everyone on campus seemed to already be gone. 'And it's not even five o'clock!' Since nearly every class taught at Mountain View College met Monday through Thursday, few of his teaching colleagues even bothered to show up on Fridays.

As he approached his Jimmy, now conspicuously visible with the parking lot near empty, Mark saw someone standing by the truck. As he walked closer, he could see that it was George Vogel.

"Well," Mark called out, "to what do I owe this pleasure?"

George waited for Mark to walk across the parking lot. "Need to talk." George replied, once Mark walked up.

"Sure. What's up?" Mark asked.

"Nothing, really, that a cold beer won't cure." George quickly assured Mark. "How about joining me for a quick one down at Rory's? That is, of course, if you don't already have plans."

Rory's was actually the local post of the Veterans of Foreign Wars. But since Rory Wilson had ran the V.F.W. since 1951, no one referred to it in any other way than simply "Rory's." Mark seldom stopped in at Rory's. He was not a veteran of a foreign war, or of any military service for that matter.

Furthermore, he was sensitive to the fact that being seen coming and going from what was generally considered the local tavern was not healthy for his professional career. Though he did enjoy a cold beer from time to time, adding to the equation was Mark's belief that all of the remaining cigarette smokers in the county met up at Rory's. Consequently, walking through the door made one's clothes, hair, and skin smell like cigarettes. A beer at Rory's seldom seemed worth the bother.

Nevertheless, Mark would not say "no" to George. "You are in luck, old man. Fact is, I don't have anything planned this evening and a cold beer sounds good."

"Great," George said. "You drive. Since the weather was so nice, I walked out here from town."

Within a few minutes, Mark was sitting across a table from George inside Rory's, drinking a cold beer and breathing near terminal amounts of carcinoma- laden air.

On the ride from Mountain View College, George had purposely remained aloft to the reason for getting together. He chose, instead, to speak about Bob Tyler's latest round of car troubles that continuously plagued the 1978 Ford he refused to trade Mark knew to allow George his way. In due time he would learn what it was George wanted to discuss.

George had always been a friend of the Benton family. After Mark's parents died, George had become even closer, making sure that a parent figure of sorts remained ever present and steadfast in Mark's life.

"So tell me," George finally said, finally getting to the point. "How are things in your life these days?"

Mark could tell from the look in George's eyes that simply saying "fine" was not going to suffice, even though things were currently good in Mark's life. Clearly, George wanted to know what had been preoccupying Mark's mind for the last several months. Mark was cornered and it was time to fess up.

"Well," Mark slowly began, "lately I have had a growing fascination surrounding an envelope that I found last January."

"What kind of envelope?" George inquired, as he shifted his weight in his chair and brought his full attention to bear.

"A rather large manila envelope," said Mark, pausing for the moment to take another drink of beer. "Do you remember a few months ago, when I moved from my basement office up to the second floor?"

"Yes."

"Well, a couple of guys from the maintenance department helped move my boxes and furniture upstairs that day. When they moved one of my file cabinets, they found an old manila envelope that had obviously fallen behind the cabinet. I assumed it was full of student assignments—I had lost a bunch of class projects sometime back and I figured it must be them. Anyway, I just set the envelope aside. When I finally got around to opening the envelope later that day, I discovered that the papers inside were not my long lost student projects."

Mark paused again, expecting George to ask about the contents of the envelope. However, George remained quiet, allowing Mark to continue telling the story at his own pace.

"What I found," continued Mark, "was a collection of writings—poetry to be exact—written by Thomas Kane, who occupied the office prior to my arrival at the college. All I can tell from the writings is that he wrote them to a woman, but I don't have a clue about the woman's name or current whereabouts."

"No clue whatsoever?" George asked thoughtfully. Mark could sense that George was systematically running through his mind every female resident that had lived in Preston Falls, CO, during the time Thomas Kane had lived there, trying to recall whether he had noticed Kane spending time with any one of them. A moment later, George made known the results of his thought.

"Kane was never seen in the company of a woman," George concluded, "during his five years in Preston Falls—least ways, not with anyone I can remember."

'If George Vogel can't remember,' thought Mark, 'then it should definitely be considered gospel!'

"Actually," said Mark, as he motioned to the waitress for another round of beers, "I got the sense this woman was nowhere near Preston Falls."

"How so?" George asked.

"Well," Mark replied, finally getting to the heart of the matter, "these were love poems, George—some of the most poignant words I have ever read. Guess that is why they have captured my fascination for the past several months. Anyway, I was able to tell from Kane's writings that he was desperately trying to convince this woman to leave the man she was with and to come spend the rest of her life with him."

"And there was no mention of the woman's name or address?" George asked.

"No," replied Mark. "And therein lays my dilemma." Before he could explain further, however, the waitress returned to their table. She smiled at Mark in an inviting, flirtatious manner, as she delivered a second round of beer. Mark dutifully thanked her. The young waitress turned and walked off displaying movement that was definitely more accentuated than a woman's natural walk should be.

"Yeah, the girls used to look at me that way," George stated in obvious reminisce.

"Oh, you know they still do!" Mark offered in an attempt to bolster George's aging ego.

"Don't bullshit me, boy," George barked in a gruff voice that lacked any meaningful bite. The men then smiled at each other, knowing that some things were universal, and talking 'trash' about manly prowess transcended age and time. "So tell me about this dilemma you have."

"Well," Mark continued, "after I read the poems—some ninety-two in all—I suddenly felt compelled to find this woman and return the poems to her."

Mark reflected a moment on his last comment. A new thought had suddenly come to mind. "Fact is," he continued, "since the poems are all handwritten, I'm not even sure he ever sent the poems to her."

George stood without warning. "Growing old can be such a pain," he said. "Hold your thought—I need to go see a man about a dog." It was with that explanation, as precise as any Mark had heard in a long while, George headed off to the men's room.

Mark began to think about this new possibility which had just come to mind. 'Is it possible,' he thought, 'that Kane never sent the poems to his beloved mystery woman?' If he had sent them, Kane would have written or somehow made another copy to send, since the old manila envelope contained original handwritten copies.

Mark recalled his conversation with Samantha Kane, where he inferred the poems were perhaps intended for Samantha's mother. Samantha had failed to share any knowledge of another woman's existence. Perhaps Samantha was simply unaware of the existence of the woman. Even though Mark believed in his heart there was a story to be told, he now wondered what the ramifications might be if Samantha were to learn of her father's secret love.

George returned and sat down. He looked at Mark from across the table in the way an adult looks at a child experiencing troubling times.

"Seems to me," he said to Mark, "you need to listen to your heart. If you think there is a story to be written, you should give it your best effort."

George shifted his weight and leaned forward. He was looking at Mark directly in the eyes.

"However," he continued, "be careful what questions you ask. To be sure, love is a part of life. If we are fortunate enough to love and to be loved. And true love can most assuredly be romantic. But the fact is, life is not always romantic. Sometimes, the deepest pain can come from the brightest love—pain felt not only by those who are in love.

Often, those who love the ones in love may feel the pain of confusion, abandonment, or betrayal."

Mark was seeing a depth to George's personality he never knew existed. What George was saying seemed to underscore Mark's own confusion and uncertainty.

"Listen to your heart." George said, as he stood and placed a one-dollar tip on the table for the young waitress. "And as a writer, be prepared to listen to the hearts of others. Do not limit yourself or your work by thinking that the obvious story is the only story. Truth is, every person's heart has a different story to tell."

That evening, Mark thought about what George had said. He found himself wrestling with both what to do and with what not to do. He glanced again at the copies he had made of Thomas Kane's writings. With that look, Mark Benton realized what his next move would be. He would wait a few weeks then give Samantha Kane another call.

Sam stared at the papers she now held in her trembling hands. There was no doubt the papers were in her father's very distinctive writing. Settling back into the softness of her couch, Sam began to read the first of what seemed to be at least a hundred pages.

"With every glance you send my way,
With smiles I so adore,
With your graceful style, you've caused me
To like you more and more.

'Lost in your fragrance and blinded by love,'
Quote poets of timeless lore;
There's not a moment I don't think
I want you more and more.

You gently give your loving touch
That moves me to the core.
You awoke a yearning deep within;
I need you more and more.

You've forever changed my life and soul;
I can't remember 'before.'
Still of all things known for which I'm sure:
I love you more and more."

Sam's mind raced. She had no doubt that these words were written by her father to Amanda. What other explanation could there be? The two envelopes seemed identical in every way, except for the words "from Amanda" written on the outside of one. She placed the first poem on the end table beside her and turned her attention to the next one.

"I awoke to find a gentle snow
In the early hours of morn.
I fought back tears of loneliness-
A crown I oft adorn.

From my bedroom window I watched the snow
Fall slowly from above.
My mind completely filled with thoughts
Of the woman that I love.

The perfume she wore earlier that day
Lingered by the bed.
'You make me feel alive again.'
Were words that she had said.

And as those words haunted my soul,
I began to wonder why
She felt she must return to him-
To a marriage doomed to die.

I remembered all our times as one,
Wondering what more there was to say.
My mind searched for perfect words
That would forever make her stay.

I know her love for me is real;
Her soft touch tells me so.
Yet one of us seeks our destiny fast,
While the other prefers it slow.

I awoke to find a gentle snow
In the early hours of morn.
I fought back tears of loneliness-
A path forever worn."

A tear fell down Sam's cheek as she gently set this poem aside. She thought about his words. Clearly, her father had been very much in love with this woman. Nevertheless, Amanda remained a puzzle, as did the details of the romance. Since her father had died alone without ever having mentioned Amanda, it seemed obvious the two had never found each other on any kind of permanent basis.

Sam continued reading her father's words—words she was surprised to learn her father was capable of writing.

"I asked for the thousandth time
To expedite our fate:
'Leave him now and come with me.'
Yet all she said was 'Wait.'

I begged her with my heart in hand,
Before it was too late,
To start a life of joy and love.
But still she said 'Let's wait.'

Soon the tears streamed down my face;
My soul had found its mate!
But as she kissed away those tears,
She could only say 'Please wait.'

My biggest fear is time will turn
My jealousy to hate.
But the more I push for her to act,
The more she says 'Let's wait.'

I know our love was meant to be;
Life's paths for us await.
I've given all there is to give;
God grant me strength to wait."

Sam wondered how long her father waited for Amanda. Did he begin his wait immediately after leaving her mother? It appeared he was still waiting for Amanda at the time of his death. Clearly, they both loved each other very much. What, then, proved stronger than love, keeping them apart for all those years? The questions in her mind seemed endless.

All through the evening, Sam read page after page—many more than once. The same words that had captured Mark Benton's heart for the past several months now captivated her heart as well. She found herself completely and utterly overwhelmed by the poignancy of it all. If certain of nothing else, she now knew she had to find Amanda. With her father gone, only Amanda could answer the multitude of questions Sam felt compelled to ask.

When Sam fell asleep that night on her living room couch, covered by the afghan her mother had made, she held in her hands the handwritten words of her father:

"There you were still looking the same
As you did the day we parted.
And there I was still longing for
The love we each discarded.

For people come and people go,
And most of them are kind.
Yet for everything a man acquires,
There's something left behind.

And what I've left for you to keep
Is a part of me doomed to die.
Please take it now and don't look back
To pause and wonder why.

For if you do, you'll realize
You hold a part of my life.
You might regret, at a time too late,
You didn't become my wife.

Just try to remember, from time to time,
For me, you were the first;
You showed me a tender way to love,
So beautifully unrehearsed."

Chapter Ten

iolets. 'What a simple, common flower,' Mark thought. 'How could anyone love them so dearly?' He was thinking, of course, of the numerous references to this wildflower found throughout the writings of Thomas Kane. As Mark walked across the small college campus, he noticed a small group of violets growing wild under an aging elm tree.

Certainly, roses yielded a high degree of "romantic clout" when it came to giving flowers as a gift. Roses were an expensive gift and were universally recognized as the flower signifying one person's love for another. As Mark stopped to look at the violets scattered about the ground, he could not help but see the flower in a different light. The simple yet unmistakable beauty of these violets now touched him in a way never before felt.

The wildflowers were added evidence that warm weather had once again arrived. The record snowfall that fell during the winter had melted and had done so at a pace that precluded any flooding. Spring was definitely in the air. However, because of the high altitude, spring in Preston Falls was always very short. Even though it was the last week in May, daytime temperatures barely broke the sixty-degree mark.

Mark was looking forward for his summer vacation this year, which, if all went as planned, would begin the following week. He was looking forward to traveling, although this year he had no particular destination in mind. Remembering back, he had always enjoyed the summer trips taken as a kid, riding in the back of his parent's huge station wagon as they made their way across country to this place or that. He had now come to realize too many summers had passed since those days with his family. Mark had decided it was time to simply load up the Jimmy and, for a few weeks, follow the road to wherever it would take him.

Mark finished his lunchtime walk, a ritual that began each year as soon as warm temperatures arrived, and returned to his office. His concerns about being located on the second floor of Riggins Hall proved to be well founded. Dr. Martha Simmons, his department chair, was forever bringing up the fact that Mark had not published anything significant for a "conspicuously long time," and members of the English Studies Department needed to set the example for the other faculty members on campus. She was always looking into his office, as though taking mental note of when he was in and what he was doing. Overall, Mark felt he was now part of a micro-managed mess most hours of the day.

Mark sat down behind his desk, which, by anyone else's standards, was piled dangerously high with student exams and assignments. Immediately, the blinking red light on the side of his telephone caught his attention. As cluttered as his desk usually stayed, a flashing red light was, in fact, about the only way for anything buried on the desk to gain Mark's attention.

'Another student seeking academic dispensation for their missing assignments,' Mark thought, with professional cynicism. Historically, there was always a rash of these calls the last week of the school semester. The excuses students gave for missing homework assignments never ceased to both amaze and humor him. Mark grabbed a pen from his shirt pocket, pulled a piece of paper at random from the closest pile, picked up the telephone, and pressed the "Voice Mail" button.

There was only one message waiting, which dutifully played back to Mark. Surprisingly, the message was not from a student, a colleague, or a friend. It was not even a message from one of those textbook marketers who incessantly tried to convince faculty to buy their textbooks over those offered by their competitors. Rather, it was a message from Samantha Kane.

Why did you call him?

It was the little voice in the back of Sam's mind. It had been asking her this same question since she left him the voice message earlier in the week. She went into the kitchen and poured herself a glass of iced tea. After smartly garnishing the beverage with a slice of lemon, she took the sweetened-to-Southern-perfection drink, slid open the patio door, and stepped outside onto her small but comfortable patio.

Why did you call him?

She sat down on a blue and white stripped patio chair, designed for relaxing in the sun, and began sipping her iced tea. The warmth of the sun felt good against her skin and she soon found her mind drifting back through the pages inside the second manila envelope.

Why did you call him?!

The voice was becoming annoying. Sam glanced at the small patio table beside her chair. The envelope Mark had sent was still lying there. Sam had spent most of the morning here, reading the pages her father had written. Drawn by a force she could neither explain nor resist, Sam again pulled the poems out of the envelope. She took another drink of iced tea, set down the glass, and began once again to read the touching words of her father.

"It's five o'clock in the morning;
The sun's about to rise.
There's frost outside the window pane,
And sorrow in your eyes.

The stars are fading quietly;
The night is almost gone.
You slowly turn away from me,
With tears to greet the dawn.

I want to kiss away your tears,
And give you back your smile.
But other voices beckon you
For just a little while.

It hurts me so to let you leave;
Your love can feel so right.
I long to lay you down again,
For just another night.

But it's once again 'Goodbye, my love.'
I'm already feeling blue.
For although there's always someone else,
There's no one else like you."

It was becoming clear that Amanda had been with someone else at the time and had been unable to give herself fully to Sam's father. Sam sensed a tremendous amount of hurt and anguish in these words. She could not help but wonder how deep his love for Amanda must have been in order for him to endure her being with someone else. Sam knew she could never tolerate such a relationship. In fact, she was certain such a situation would be sufficient reason to stop loving someone, a certainty that presupposed one could simply stop loving.

But why did you call him?

Sam set the poem aside and picked up another from the stack. She was not yet ready to answer the voice inside her head.

"At four in the morning, I lie alone;
It's still too dark to see.
Yet all the approaching dawn awakes
Is the painful mourning in me.

My shadow lies close where you once lay;
The moon glows in the dark.
The space is empty outside my door,
Where often you would park.

The room still echoes with your voice;
The hours are painfully long.
I spend my time now wondering why
Our love turned out so wrong.

For the thousandth time, I ask myself,
'Can't we control our fate?'
Yet the answer's all too obvious:
For us, it's much too late.

The clock strikes six; it's time to rise,
I sense the morning sun.
Once more the daylight hides the night
From this lonely marriage of one."

Sam could see similarity between Amanda's words and her father's words. In both cases, many of the poems spoke of the deep love each felt for the other. However, there were also poems, like the one just read, which described the painful agony and hopelessness of love lost. What remained unclear to Sam was the chronology of their writings to each other. Since none of the poems bore any dates, Sam remained unsure when they met, how long they loved, and when they went their separate ways—and why, for that matter. Of one thing, however, Sam was sure—she desperately needed to find the answers.

Is that why you called him? Do you think he has the answers?

Sam sipped her iced tea and pulled another sheet of paper from the envelope Mark had sent.

"You've left my life, and in your place
Emptiness has returned.
Alone, I wonder what was the cost
Of all that I have learned.

By tenderly catching me with your smile,
You kept my heart inspired.
Why then has our time together
Left me sad and tired?

Perhaps it's fear that turned you back
To walk life's lonely road.
So much was there for us to share:
Now stories left untold.

Yet, the loneliness left reminds to me
I've been this way before.
And as with me, then so with love:
An encounter nevermore."

Sam began looking about for a tissue to wipe tears which suddenly ran down her cheeks. She found a used tissue absently stuck between the cushions of the patio chair and wiped her face. It was proving very difficult for her to understand her father's passion for this woman named Amanda—a passion so strong he seemed willing to live his life alone if it could not be lived with the woman he loved.

Why do you think he has the answers to your questions?

Sam was not sure she even knew the questions she wanted to ask. Furthermore, she was not certain how understanding her father's life would help her to understand her own. Yet, she just could not let it go. For the last several months, the story that had been unfolding before her eyes and it now seemed too powerful to deny. Sam let out a sigh, only to have it be quickly carried away by the gentle afternoon breeze. She selected another of her father's poems to read.

"Softly falls the snow outside;
Alone, I spend my time.
It seems I've tried my entire life
To make my feelings rhyme.

I realize now I've lost my love,
A love I thought was mine.
And in her haste to leave that day,
She left unfinished wine.

The room still echoes with the sounds
Of now so distant laughter.
We'd drank the wine and promised our love,
For then, and ever after.

Yet she is gone; the wine remains
To remind me she was there.
I now must take my wine and search
For someone who will care.

I've made this trip alone before;
I hope it won't take long.
And if I find another love,
I'll sing to her this song:

'I'll promise to drink all of yours,
If you'll drink all of mine:
For no longer can I bear the taste
Of love's unfinished wine.' "

Sam closed her eyes. She remembered how funny her father had seemed when she was a young girl. He always had some stupid joke waiting in the wings which he could seemingly apply to any situation. Now, years later, as she read her father's most intimate thoughts, he was appearing more as a man who had used humor to mask his pain and anguish.

Sam decided she was not up to reading anymore this particular afternoon. Perhaps a nap would help put things in a better perspective. Slowly, she drifted off to sleep under the warmth of the Texas sun.

Just give him time… he will call.

As Mark stared across the room, he suddenly realized the automated attendant was repeatedly instructing him to "press 'K' to keep the current message, press 'D' to delete the current message, press 'P' to play the message again, or press 'F' to forward the message to another voice-mail box." He pressed "P", and the message replayed.

> "*Message received Monday*, *May 29th, 9:42 AM*..... Hi, Mark. This is Samantha Kane calling. I wanted to thank you for sending the envelope containing my father's writings. I would be less than honest if I didn't say this material has certainly taken me by surprise. It has served to balance and compliment the other envelope I found while packing up my father's office several years ago. Anyway, I now find myself wondering if there is some merit to your idea that there may be a story in all of this. Perhaps you could give me a call, if you are still interested that is, and we can discuss the idea further. Thanks again for sending the papers."

Before the automated attendant began its instructions once again, Mark pressed "K" to archive the message. He returned the telephone receiver to its cradle, stood, and began pacing about his office. His mind was racing.

"Damn!" Mark exclaimed aloud, realizing Samantha had left the message five days earlier on Monday morning.

'How could I not have seen the light blinking all week?' Mark asked himself in exasperation. The only thing he could figure was that part of the perpetual mess inhabiting the top of his desk had somehow obscured the light on the side of his telephone and had done so successfully for five days.

"And," Mark said aloud, "what does she mean by the other envelope? What other envelope?!"

Mark remembered every word of their telephone conversation and Samantha Kane had not mentioned the existence of another envelope. The thought of another old manila envelope full of Thomas Kane's writings excited Mark to no end. All he could think about now was asking Samantha if he could read them.

Mark sat back down at his desk, pulled opened the center drawer, and hurriedly began to inspect each small piece of paper he returned. Samantha's telephone number was inscribed on one of these small morsels and he could not find it fast enough.

Then, suddenly, there it was, written on the back of a bookstore receipt for two packs of AAA batteries. Samantha Kane 921-375-7118. Mark had no problem justifying in his mind that the call was business-related and dialed Samantha's number from his office telephone. He was immediately relieved to hear it ring on the other end.

'Why isn't someone answering the phone?' Sam thought. The sound seemed to come closer with each ring. Suddenly she awoke, startled by the portable phone ringing beside her. 'This had better be good!' she thought, as she reached for the phone.

"Hello," she answered in a flat, monotone voice.

"Hi, Samantha?" a young man on the other end asked.

Sam immediately recognized Mark's deep and undeniably sensual voice.

I told you he would call.

"Yes," she answered, her voice overtly perking up a bit.

"Hi! It's Mark Benton returning your call."

"Oh, hi, Mark," she replied, quickly softening her voice for no apparent reason. "Glad you returned my call."

"Well," Mark said, "I must apologize for taking so long to get back to you. This has been the last week of the semester and, what with final exams and everything, I…"

"No problem." Sam interjected. "I remember those days well! I was so glad to get school behind me. Now, if I ever get my student loans behind me, I can really start to live!"

"That goes for you and me both!" Mark replied with a chuckle. "And, given our chosen professions, I'd be willing to bet you get yours paid off long before I do mine!"

"Oh, I don't know about that!" said Sam. "I sometimes think the whole federal loan process is designed so we never pay them off!"

"Well, perseverance has always been my motto," Mark said, recalling the words prominently displayed on his office wall. "I really do believe all good things come to those who wait."

"Can I hold you to that?" Sam said in a slightly flirtatious tone that flew out of her mouth without warning.

What are you doing?

"I suppose I can allow you to hold me to it," Mark replied with an equal measure of familiarity in his voice.

Sam was again surprised at the ease with which she could converse with this man whom she had never met. She had been quite relaxed the first time they talked over the telephone and she felt even more at ease this time. However, small talk was not bringing the conversation around to the point.

"Mark," she began slowly in a more serious tone, "now that I have had the opportunity to read my father's writings, I am wondering if perhaps there just might be a story here. You had mentioned that possibility the last time we spoke."

"Well," Mark said cautiously, "Whether or not there is a story of interest to others depends. At first, I did think there might be a story, what with finding a lost envelope full of love poems. Now, however, I am not so sure. There are so many details missing. If I fill in those blanks with my own assumptions, it might make for a good story, but it could very well end up being pure fiction. I continue to hope that the story—if one does exist—could be a true story of romance and unfulfilled love, making it more meaningful somehow. As it stands right now, I am not sure how to fill in the missing pieces without some investigative work. I do think if I could read the other set of your father's writings, I would have a better sense for the context in which everything was written."

Mark's last statement immediately went over Sam's head. "You lost me," she said. "What other writings of my father are you talking about?"

Now Mark was confused. "The writings you mentioned in the voice mail you left me last Monday—the writings you found when you packed up your father's office three years ago."

"Those weren't my father's writings," Sam quickly clarified. "What I found was an old manila envelope containing her writings."

"Her writings?" repeated Mark, his mind suddenly in high gear. "Do you mean your mother?"

The thought of her mother writing the things Amanda had written struck Sam as absurdly comical. She briefly laughed aloud before setting the record straight.

"Heavens, no!" she exclaimed. "And nothing against my mother, but she is just not the type to put those kinds of feelings into words. And even if she were, I doubt she would write them about my father!"

Mark had suspected all along that the woman Thomas Kane had loved so deeply was probably someone other than Samantha's mother. He just did not want to be the one to say it first. Now that Samantha had crossed that bridge, Mark was quick to follow.

"Do you mind if I ask her name?" Mark asked.

"Her name," Sam said, "is Amanda."

So there it was. Amanda. Mark now had a name to add to the story. Perhaps this would mean that soon he would have a face to put with the images in his mind. Knowing her name did very little, however, to ebb the growing intrigue that surrounded the existence of another envelope.

"Do you know Amanda's last name? Do you know where she is now? Did the two of them ever get together? What did she write to your father?" Mark's questions came more quickly than Sam could answer.

"Slow down!" Sam interjected, realizing for the first time how captivated Mark seemed to be with her father's writings. The sincerity of his interest touched her heart. "Let me take you through what little I know about all of this."

For the next thirty minutes or so, Sam told Mark the story of her father divorcing her mother and leaving them when she was fifteen years old. She explained how she and her father continued to have a good relationship over the years, in spite of her parents failed marriage. She had often asked him, especially after he moved to Colorado, if he was seeing anyone special. She had done so as a surreptitious gesture to let him know it was fine with her if he moved on with his life. However, he had always responded to her by saying the "only woman in his life is you."

Sam continued her story, with Mark hanging on her every word. She explained how she had found an old manila envelope in her father's office, an envelope that bore the words "from Amanda" written in her father's very neat and unmistakable handwriting. She tried to describe the twenty-eight poems found inside the envelope, words that Amanda had written to her father. Not surprisingly though, Sam found it difficult to convey the essence of Amanda's writing.

"Each poem Amanda wrote," Sam explained, "described the incredible love she felt for my father. At the same time, each reinforced an inevitable conclusion that for some unknown reason the two were doomed to live their lives apart."

"Did you ever learn Amanda's last name or her whereabouts?" Mark asked.

"I'm afraid not," Sam answered. "The only thing I am relatively sure of is that the two of them never ended up together. I'm sure my father would have told me had their love survived."

"Are you sure," Mark countered, "that their love didn't survive?"

Sam was not sure what Mark was trying to say. "What do you mean?" she asked.

"Well," replied Mark, "what if their love never died? What if there were reasons other than the possible demise of their love that kept them apart? I mean, Shakespeare's Romeo and Juliet is a story of one of the greatest loves ever known and the two of them never got together."

"I hardly think the writings of an old man can be considered in the same league as Romeo and Juliet!" Sam responded. "So I'm still not sure I see your point."

"My point," Mark clarified, "is that perhaps Amanda is still out there somewhere, still harboring a tremendous love for your father. If she could be located, there might very well be a story to be told—a story which might inspire readers to seize love when it happens and to not let the realities of life stand in the way of love's promise for mutual fulfillment."

He does have a way with words, doesn't he?

Sam sensed where this was going and knew that soon there would be no stopping it. But deep inside she also knew she did not want to stop it.

"I suppose you're right, Mark," she answered. "but I'm really not sure how to find Amanda without knowing her last name. Do you have any ideas?"

"Well," he continued, "I would like to first read what Amanda wrote to your father. I know you've read them— probably as many times as I've read your father's words— but perhaps a fresh pair of eyes might find some clue to Amanda's whereabouts that you've missed."

"Sure." Sam replied. "I don't mind sharing them with you. Besides, if it weren't for your interest, I would have never seen my father's writings. Would you like for me to mail them to you?"

Mark's thoughts were suddenly derailed. Out of nowhere, he heard the words of George Vogel. 'Listen to you heart', George had told him. Then, just as quickly and before he could take the time to mentally enumerate all the reasons why he should not be speaking them, the words flew out of Mark's mouth.

"Actually, Samantha," he said in a nonchalant manner, "I plan on being in the Houston area later next week. It is a part of my summer vacation route this year, and I would love to take the time to meet you. Perhaps I could take you to dinner one evening and we could discuss all of this in detail. If you're agreeable, I could wait to read Amanda's writings until then."

Sam certainly did not see this one coming. Mark was going to be in Houston next week. In addition, he wanted to meet her. Yet even with all her bad experiences over the past few years, none of a litany of blind date horror stories came to mind.

Isn't this what you wanted?

"I'd like that," was all Sam could say. For Mark, it was all he wanted to hear. The two made plans to e-mail each other the details of when, where, and how they would meet. Finally, their goodbyes were said, leaving both to their own thoughts of the other.

Sam could not help but notice how incredibly beautiful the sunset suddenly seemed that evening.

Be careful what you ask for; you just might get it.

As she turned and walked back inside her condominium, Sam thought for a fleeting second that the voice inside her head was not her own—she began to think it belonged to her father.

Chapter Eleven

lasses were finally over at Mountain View College with the spring semester coming to an end. Students had packed their things and were going their separate ways, returning to friends, families, or in some cases to the recreational retreats scattered throughout the great wilderness known as the Rockies. The emptiness grew louder with each departing student, until it entombed the campus in an eerie quiet found only during those few times when students were away.

Residents of Preston Falls looked forward to this time and would dutifully reclaim the town as their very own, albeit for only a short while. More local folks could now be seen walking the town's streets. With the evenings warming as summer approached, they strolled through the town's small park, stopping to sit inside the gazebo or on the park benches previously commandeered by young couples who sought a break from their academic environment and taciturn resident halls.

Mark spent most of his Saturday grading final exams. By late in the afternoon he had put his grade rosters in a sealed envelope and had slid them under the campus registrar's door. He spent his Sunday cleaning house, mowing the lawn, paying bills, and packing for his trip. Since he was not sure exactly how long he would be gone, Mark decided to take most of his modest wardrobe. He thought it would be better to have too much, than to not have enough.

On Monday, Mark started the day early, loading up his Jimmy in his usual, highly organized manner. He checked the air pressure in the tires, inspected the engine's fluid levels, and made sure his maps were strategically positioned on the seat beside him for easy access. By 8:00 AM, he was ready to go. He backed the Jimmy out of his driveway and began what he hoped would prove to be a very rewarding trip. As he headed out of Preston Falls, Mark saw George Vogel's car parked outside Mandy's Café. He parked the Jimmy in the space next to George's car and went inside to tell George about the last minute plans to drive to Houston.

To Mark's delight, George was sitting at the back table alone. It was late enough that some of the group had already come and gone, yet early enough that others in the group had not arrived. George smiled as Mark pulled out a chair and sat down.

"Morning, boy," George said. "So what's on your agenda for today, seeing as how school is out for the summer?"

"Actually," Mark replied slowly, "I am on my way out of town for a while."

"Really? Where are you off to?" George asked, sensing there was more to this story than just a few days of recreation.

"Houston, Texas," Mark answered.

While George mulled over Mark's response, Jenny brought over freshly brewed coffee, poured Mark a cup, and gave George his third refill of the morning. George looked intently into Mark's eyes and it was there he found his answer.

"Going to see the girl—what's her name—Samantha Kane?" he asked.

Mark immediately gave George his famous Benton smile. "Yes, I am," he answered. For the next few minutes, Mark brought George up to speed on every new detail of the story, including the existence of a second envelope which contained the writings of a woman named Amanda.

Once he heard these new details, George was quick to give Mark his blessing. Truth be known, that's exactly why Mark had stopped at Mandy's on his way out of town.

"I think you should go for the story," George affirmed. "It's not every day we get an opportunity to become a part of such an intriguing story involving the human spirit. I am interested in learning how this all turns out. Hell, if a gruff old codger like myself is interested, then maybe other folks might be interested as well. You just be careful out there on the road."

"Thanks, George," Mark said. He was glad to know he had the support of his older friend.

As they rose from the table and shook hands, George offered his final words of advice. "Just remember what I told you," he began. "Listen to your heart. But as a writer, you must also listen to the hearts of others. Don't limit yourself or your work by thinking that the obvious story is the only story."

"I do remember what you told me," Mark assured him and offered George a direct quote as a testament to his memory. "'Every person's heart has a different story to tell.'" George simply nodded, as Mark turned to leave.

As he drove out of Preston Falls that morning and began the thirteen hundred mile journey to Houston, Mark contemplated many things. He thought of his parents and wondered if their love had been as deep and as meaningful as the love between Thomas and Amanda. He thought about what questions he would ask Amanda once he had located her. Moreover, and much to his surprise, he found himself thinking about another woman he had not yet met—a young woman named Samantha Kane.

For the past few days, Sam had kept to herself the most recent conversation with Mark Benton. She did not even tell her close friend Marcy that she had called him. Now, with Mark on his way to Houston, she realized it was probably better that she did tell her. And she could just about guess how Marcy was going to react.

But before she called her friend, Sam decided to first call Paul at work. She caught him moments after he arrived in his office. She hoped he would be in a more benevolent mood this early in the day, since she was catching him before the challenges of project management had a chance to manifest. She told him she wanted to take a week or so off from work and asked if current project schedules would allow her to do so. Paul grumbled a few half-hearted reservations, but, in the end, said it would be okay. Sam made sure to tell him that she would not be checking her e-mail during her time off. If something came up, it would just have to wait.

Next, she dialed Marcy's home number. It rang only once, but Marcy's voice instantly gave away the fact that she had been sleeping in.

"Hello." answered a voice, struggling for consciousness.

"Marcy, it's me," Sam answered in an overly chipper tone. "It's about time you got your lazy butt out of bed!"

"Girl," Marcy began with a groan, "if you only knew what kind of night I had, you wouldn't be calling so damn early, nor would you be expecting my butt to get out of bed!"

"Early?" Sam asked, smiling to herself.

"Yes, early!" Marcy replied. "Eric came over last night, and well, he ended up spending the night. Suffice it to say, the man is terminally insatiable. I might very well never walk the same again! I don't think I got three hours sleep the entire night."

"Well, there you go!" Sam said in obvious support of a night well spent. "Listen, you know I wouldn't be calling this early if it weren't important."

As Marcy responded, "Yeah, yeah, so what's up?", Sam could hear her banging around in her kitchen in an effort to make her morning coffee.

Sam had already filled Marcy in on the details of the manila envelope she had found in Colorado shortly after her father died, including what she knew about her father's secret love. Marcy also knew about the recent call and subsequent envelope from Mark Benton.

"Remember a few weeks ago, when I received the envelope from Professor Benton in Preston Falls, Colorado?"

"Yes," Marcy replied as she filled the coffee maker with water.

"Well," Sam continued, "I sort of called him last week."

"'Sort of' called him?" Marcy teased. "Seems to me that's like being pregnant—you either are or you aren't. So, you either called him or you didn't. Which is it?"

"Okay—I called him," Sam confessed. "I read through my father's writings several times, the one's Mark Benton mailed, and I think there might be a story in all of this. As a matter of fact, he was the one who mentioned the idea of a story when he first called me—said he was looking to write an article."

"Yeah, so…" prompted Marcy, in a tone reflecting obvious impatience.

"So," continued Sam, "I called him and I agreed to help him write an article."

"That sounds great, Sam," Marcy said flatly, "but couldn't you have just sent me an e-mail to tell me this wonderful news?"

"Well, I suppose I could have," Sam replied coyly, "but I thought you might want to talk about his arriving in Houston tomorrow."

"What," exclaimed Marcy, her interest suddenly aroused, "he's coming here?"

"I asked him if he wanted me to mail him what Amanda had written," Sam explained, her words now coming much faster. "But then he said he was going to be in the Houston area, and would I mind if he stopped by, and perhaps we could talk about everything over dinner, and, oh, Marcy, tell me I'm not making a big mistake!"

"Well, let's just step back and take a look at this," replied Marcy, carefully measuring her words. "First of all, is he single?"

"Yes," Sam confirmed. "We later discussed via e-mail when he would arrive. He mentioned that because he was single, his vacation plans were flexible."

"Does he know you're available?" Marcy asked next.

"Who says I'm available?" Sam retorted with mock indignation. "If you must know, I did mention that since

I was single, getting together over dinner would not be a problem."

"Well, there you have it!" said Marcy in a somewhat sly tone. "That's what I'm talking about! And you did say he had a sexy voice."

"No," corrected Sam, "I said he had a sensual voice."

"Same difference," Marcy continued. "So that's two points. Now, let's see what else we have here. Besides being single and having a sexy telephone voice, he enjoys romantic stories, he's educated, he's gainfully employed, you told me he was your age, and, you told me he lost his parents years ago, which means there would be no interfering mother-in-law. Hmmm… that is five more points, bringing the total to seven—and that is seven big points sight unseen! Yep, I'd say you're doing the right thing here."

"You," Sam conceded, "are hopeless. Absolutely, positively impossible. I don't know why I even bother to ask!"

Marcy laughed aloud. "Because," she countered, "you know I'm usually right. Besides, I would never steer my best friend wrong!"

"Well," Sam said, "I just hope you are right. He is supposed to be here late tomorrow afternoon. I thought we would go to Juan Pablo's for dinner—you know, give him a taste of Texas since he's been hibernating up in the Rocky Mountains for so long!"

Marcy could not help but chide Sam one last time. "They say mountain men have ferocious appetites when they come down out of the snow!"

"Yeah, well, he's buying," said Sam, bringing Marcy's obvious reference to sex back to food and dining out. "So I don't care how big an appetite he has."

"I expect a full report the first chance you get," Marcy added. "Just be yourself and I am sure he will enjoy every minute with you!"

"Thanks, Marcy," replied Sam. "Wish me luck!"

Sam spent the remainder of the morning cleaning and doing laundry. As she moved about doing her chores, she found herself wondering what Mark Benton would look like. Will he be as tall as she? And what color of eyes does he have? Sam believed a person's eyes said more about themselves than any other physical characteristic. In short, she believed that entire conversations were possible between two people by solely gazing into each other's eyes.

She thought about the moment when Amanda and her father first looked into each other's eyes. She could only imagine where they might have been. And had it been love at first sight? Her father did question, in one of his poems, how anyone could ever profess to be in love, while not having fallen in love at first sight. Sam wondered if she might know that feeling someday.

Shortly after lunch, Sam's telephone rang. She expected it to be Marcy, with another round of positive points to add to a growing list of reasons why Sam should be meeting with Mark. She grabbed her cell phone and plopped down on her favorite chair.

"Hello," she said.

"Samantha?" Emily Kane was calling to check on her beloved daughter.

"Hi, Mom!" Sam replied. "Is everything okay?"

"Everything is fine, dear," her mother replied. "I just wanted to see if you were home. I made a couple batches of coconut macaroons this morning and thought I'd bring some over to you—that is, if you'd like to have some."

Coconut macaroon cookies were only Sam's favorite cookie of all. However, as much trouble as they were to make, she seldom had the time, energy, or the talent for that matter, to make them in her own kitchen. The prospect of enjoying a batch of those tasty cookies made fresh from her mother's kitchen was simply too tempting to decline.

"Mother!" exclaimed Sam. "You know how much I adore your coconut macaroons. Are you coming over now or do I have to come and get them?!"

"I'll be over in a few minutes," Emily replied. "Have some coffee ready."

Sam promised she would have fresh coffee waiting and said goodbye. She was genuinely glad her mother was dropping by and especially pleased she was bringing her favorite treat. She quickly started a pot of coffee and walked outside to check her mail. True to her word, Emily Kane drove up as Sam was closing the mailbox door. Once she exited from the car, Sam gave her mother a hug and the two of them walked inside.

"I'll pour the coffee," Sam said, "and you get out the cookies. I haven't had any lunch so I'm ready to get down to business!"

"You sound as though you're ready to eat the entire batch!" Emily said, obviously delighted that her cooking could still evoke such excitement.

"I just might," countered Sam as the two sat down at the small kitchen table. "So, what's the occasion?"

"No occasion," replied Emily. "I just thought the two of us might share some 'girl talk.' What's new with you these days?"

Sam's first reaction to that question was, of course, thoughts of Mark Benton and the envelope he had sent to her. However, realizing her mother knew nothing about either, Sam quickly decided she had no desire to bring up the issue of her father's love for another woman. She could not see how it would serve any purpose to tell her mother. However, her hesitation in answering Emily Kane's question proved to be an open proclamation that something new was in fact going on in Sam's life. Her mother wasted no time moving in for the kill.

"Sam?" she said in a very parental, you'd-better-tell-me-now-because-you're-going-to-have-to-tell-me-sooner-or-later tone of voice.

Sam was cornered. How did this happen?! She had gone from having a well-kept secret to now having to tell her mother everything—all in the span of a couple of seconds.

'It must have been my hesitation,' she thought. 'Make a mental note to practice more immediate responses in the future!' Emily Kane waited patiently for Sam's answer, as she stirred a small portion of non-dairy creamer into her coffee.

"This is not going to be a simple story," Sam said finally. "Are you sure you want to hear it?"

"Of course I do, dear," Emily replied. "Just start at the beginning. Before you know it, it will all be told and you'll feel much better for having confided in your mother." Emily was thinking this would simply be another story of a recent date gone bad and she was prepared to give her daughter the proverbial 'there's more fish in the sea' story.

'I hope you're right,' Sam thought, as an uneasy feeling swelled inside her. Still, against her better judgment, Sam began to tell her mother the story she had kept from her the last several years. She began with how she had found the manila envelope containing what a woman named Amanda had written to her father.

As Sam spoke, Emily Kane sat quietly, listening to every word without interrupting. Sam described how Mark Benton had first contacted her. She went on to explain how he, too, had found an envelope. She told her mother how Mark had sent her the second envelope and tried to describe her surprise when she learned that the second envelope contained the writings of her father, words he had written to Amanda.

Finally, she related the most recent conversations between her and Mark, including the fact that she would be meeting him tomorrow to discuss the possibility of his writing a story concerning the whole affair. And as soon as she used the word "affair", Sam suddenly wished she had picked a better word.

"Well, that's pretty much all I know," Sam finally concluded. "Would you like to see any of the writings?"

"No," Emily replied softly, obviously deep in thought.

Sam looked hard into her mother's eyes. She was desperately hoping she had not hurt her mother by sharing these revelations. When Emily shifted her gaze and looked back at her daughter, Sam saw an expression other than hurt—an expression that seemed closer to realization. It was though her mother suddenly understood a past memory—something which had not made much sense before now.

"This is all quite curious." Emily said softly.

"Yes," Sam confirmed, suddenly struck by the possibility that her mother's reaction seemed to indicate she might know her. "Does any of this mean anything to you?"

Emily gazed out the kitchen window, as she sorted through her thoughts and memories. Sam remained patient and for the moment, deciding to pour more coffee for them both in lieu of asking more questions.

"I think it was just before Christmas," Emily slowly began to recall, "the year your father died, that I received a telephone call one afternoon. It was a woman, who explained to me she had just received back a letter she had mailed to your father. According to this woman, the letter had been returned by the post office and was stamped "undeliverable." The woman said she had tried to call him, but a heavy snowstorm had brought the telephone lines down. As I am sure you remember, there were times during bad winters when you couldn't get through on the telephone to your father for days."

Sam nodded.

"Well," Emily continued, "the woman seemed quite upset at not being able to contact him, although she did apologize for bothering me. Somehow she had known I was his ex-wife and she thought I might be able to help her locate him. She said it was very important she contact him as soon as possible. When I told her your father had died a few weeks earlier, there was a brief silence before the line went dead. She simply hung up without saying another word. She never called me again and I never knew why she was trying to contact him."

Now Sam's mind was racing. "Do you think," she asked her mother, "there might be some connection between that call and all of this?"

Emily looked up at her daughter and spoke with absolute certainty. "I know there is, dear." she replied. "The woman introduced herself to me as 'Amanda'."

Chapter Twelve

fternoon rush hour traffic was in full swing, as Mark drove into the Houston metropolitan area. To compound his frustration, there seemed little worth listening to on the radio, given the endless stream of country music and Spanish language commentary, neither of which Mark really understood. Still, Mark knew he should count his blessings.

For the most part, the trip from Preston Falls to Houston had been uneventful. The entire 1,262-mile trip had taken him through portions of Colorado, New Mexico, and Texas, where each passing mile of highway often seemed identical to the last. Mark had driven 828 miles the first day, before spending the night at a roadside motel outside Childress, Texas. Today, on his second day of travel, Mark had driven the remaining 434 miles to Houston, but only to arrive in Houston at the worst possible time.

According to the instructions and directions Samantha had provided, they were to meet at a restaurant located close to the center of the city at 6:00 PM. Fortunately, Mark soon discovered that the deeper he drove into the city, the better traffic seemed to flow—at least in his direction. At this hour of the day, more people were leaving the city of Houston than were entering. After two wrong turns and a quickly changed attempt to drive down a one-way street in the wrong direction, he found himself at Juan Pablo's Restaurant in the heart of Houston.

Mark glanced at his watch and saw that it was 6:06 PM. He parked the Jimmy in an available space, turned off the engine, and dutifully patted the dashboard in appreciation.

"You came through for me again, old girl," Mark said aloud. With over 100,000 miles on the aging truck, it was always worth a moment of celebration when the vehicle made a trip without breaking down. Mark glanced into the mirror and saw that his short hair still appeared presentable. He then took a deep breath, climbed out of the truck, and walked into the restaurant. He could feel his heart beat faster with each step he took.

"Will there just be one this evening, Sir?"

The girl smiling from behind the reservation podium was talking to Mark. She was speaking English, but with a combination of both Texan and Hispanic accents. It was more than Mark could understand during his first few moments in the Houston area.

"I'm sorry?" he politely asked in his slow, Rocky Mountain manner.

"Will you be dining alone this evening, Sir?" the hostess asked more slowly.

"Oh, uh, no," Mark stammered. "I'm supposed to meet someone."

"What is the name on the reservation?" she asked next. "I will check to see if your party has already been seated."

"Kane," Mark replied. "Samantha Kane."

The hostess quickly scanned a list of names, turned to a young waitress who had suddenly appeared and said, "Table 16." Turning back to Mark, the hostess smiled. "Enjoy your dinner, Sir."

Mark followed the waitress through a maze of people who appeared to be celebrating everything from birthdays and anniversaries to simply the opportunity of enjoying a meal out. As he walked, his mind began to race. He could not recall ever feeling this apprehensive about meeting someone. Samantha had seemed quite nice on the phone—very well educated in fact—but, what if...

"Here you are, Sir."

Mark's thoughts were suddenly cut short, as the waitress stopped at the designated table.

"I'll be back in a moment to take your orders," she said, leaving Mark standing beside the table alone.

During the past several weeks, when Mark tried to imagine how Samantha Kane would look, he found himself hoping only that she would not be unattractive. When Samantha Kane looked up and their eyes met for the first time, Mark's heart nearly stopped. Simply stated, Samantha was the most beautiful woman he had ever met.

Samantha was wearing a perfectly fitted, lightweight summer dress. The thin straps of the dress revealed well-tanned shoulders that on this particular occasion served to support her long, light brown hair. Her hazel eyes, bright as any Mark had ever looked into, began to sparkle when she smiled up at him.

Sam's smile was one of relief. She, too, had tried to imagine how he would look. Often, those who sound a certain way on the telephone look completely different than imagined when met for the first time. This, however, was not the case with Mark Benton. He was tall, which seemed to support his athletic build perfectly. However, his other features were suddenly lost, when his brown eyes met hers.

With his signature smile, he had immediately captivated her heart.

"Samantha?" he asked in a distinctive voice Sam immediately recognized.

"Hi, Mark!" she answered, hoping her voice did not seem too anxious. "It's so nice to finally meet you." Sam remained seated, extending her hand in a cordial manner.

"It's a pleasure to meet you," Mark said, as he took her outstretched hand in his. The softness and warmth of her touch sent an unexpected rush though his body. They shook hands with a somewhat less than business-like grip and Mark sat down opposite Sam.

The next two hours seemed to pass in record time. The food was wonderful and their conversation seemed almost too natural. Mark listened while Sam talked about her education, her work, and her life in the Houston area. Sam, in turn, listened while Mark talked about life in Preston Falls. She was particularly amused by his descriptions of the old timers whose lives seemed to revolve around a place called "Mandy's Café."

All too soon it seemed, the waitress made her final stop at their table. She asked if there was anything more she could get for the two of them and, upon hearing "no," left the check. Much to Mark's surprise, Sam snatched up the bill.

"No, here, let me get that," he insisted.

"I dare say you've spent enough money in the last two days just getting yourself here," Sam countered. "So I insist, let me pick up dinner."

"That's very thoughtful of you," Mark conceded. "It's been a long time since I've been treated to dinner by a woman. And, why do I get the feeling that offering to go "Dutch" is not an option?"

Sam returned his smile with one of her very best. "Because," she flatly replied, "it's not!"

"You know, Samantha," Mark said on a more serious note, "we have not yet talked about the writings."

Sam suddenly realized how unimportant the writings had become during the last two hours. Furthermore, it scared her to think how interesting she found Mark Benton to be. His comment brought her back to the purpose of their meeting.

"Yes, I know," she replied. Sam had brought a copy of Amanda's writings with her to the restaurant, but she had left it in her car. If Mark Benton had proved less interesting— or worse, had acted in a manner that made her question his character—she could have held up her end of the arrangement by simply passing along the copies to him as they left.

But he had been interesting. Even more, she found herself interested in him.

"Mark," she continued, suddenly unsure where the words were coming from, "it's still early. Would you like to follow me home and see Amanda's writings this evening? Or, would you rather meet again tomorrow sometime? I'm not working any software projects this week, so my schedule is flexible."

There was no hesitation in Mark's reply. "This evening would be great!" he quickly answered, as they stood up to leave. "Lead the way."

While Sam paid for the dinner, Mark waited at the front door. It only took a few moments for her to catch up with him and when she did, she gave him another smile.

"Thanks again for dinner," Mark told her.

"My pleasure," Sam assured him. "I don't live far, so you shouldn't have any trouble following."

When he opened the front door for her and they walked out into the fresh evening air, Mark noticed, for the first time, the perfume she was wearing. The fragrance seemed to perfectly fit both her beauty and her charm. He thought about commenting on how wonderful she smelled.

'Oh, yeah, right!' Mark thought as he walked Sam to her car. 'Just tell her she smells real good… that ought to score a lot of points!' Instead of embarrassing himself by making a stupid comment regarding her perfume, Mark chose to play it safe.

"Nice car," he said, as he opened the door of her sporty convertible.

"Thanks," Sam replied. "What are you driving, so I don't lose you?"

"I'll be in that real dirty Jimmy over there," Mark said, pointing to his truck.

"Great!" she said. "See you again in a few minutes."

With Mark following close behind, Sam pulled out of the restaurant and headed north. Her home was about a ten-minute drive and the route they were taking was straightforward.

As she drove along the well-lit streets, her thoughts seemed to jump from one thing to the next. Was she doing the right thing allowing Mark to follow her home? Was there a story surrounding the writings between Amanda and her father? Would Mark be able to help her learn the identity and whereabouts of Amanda? Was this the beginning of a meaningful friendship between Mark and herself? Sam realized that the questions she was asking herself were all the very things she was hoping would happen.

Sam turned onto her street and soon brought her convertible to a stop in her driveway. In turn, Mark brought his truck to a stop in front of her residence. During the short drive from the restaurant, Mark's thoughts had returned to the envelope of writings he had come over a thousand miles to see. If what he was about to read was anything like what he had already seen, there would be no denying his passion to write this story.

Furthermore, it would certainly demand his speaking with Amanda, so he could learn all the details of this deeply loving relationship firsthand. It would also mean he would need to have Samantha Kane's involvement and blessing. Mark hoped that by the end of the evening, he would know the answer on both counts.

"Be it ever so humble," Sam said, as they walked up the sidewalk to the front door.

"It looks like a wonderful neighborhood," Mark assured her, as he quickly looked at the adjacent residences.

"It is a nice area," she replied, "and, it's close to my mother. All things considered, I'm quite comfortable where I'm at."

Sam unlocked the door, entered and turned on the lights.

"Please make yourself comfortable," she said, pointing to the living room. "Would you like a glass of wine? I have a bottle of pinot noir that I have been saving for a special occasion."

"A glass of pinot would be great," answered Mark, as he walked into Sam's living room. His eyes immediately began taking in all of the many trinkets strategically placed about that define a person's interests, tastes and ultimately their personality.

There were numerous matted prints hanging about the living room that reflected a conservative, yet warm, living environment. He also saw that the living room was home to numerous books, all placed neatly into bookcases that lined one entire wall. With his professional curiosity aroused, he walked to the bookshelves to see what sort of titles Samantha Kane read. Not surprisingly, this articulate woman read a combination of classic literature, contemporary non-fiction, and, much to his personal delight, best-selling romantic novels.

As he continued to look about the room, Mark next noticed some pictures resting on a mantel. He walked over to the fireplace and looked at each photo. Some were obvious pictures from Samantha's childhood; others were group pictures of family or friends. One photo caught Mark's attention, and he picked up the framed picture. It was a photograph of Samantha standing with her arm around an older man.

"That's my father," Sam said, as she walked up from behind. She handed Mark his wine.

Mark was looking at Thomas Kane for the first time. Dr. Thomas Kane—teacher, father, and, yes, poet. Although he was smiling in the picture, the look in Thomas Kane's eyes suggested he was somewhat less than a happy individual. Mark was not quite sure how to read the look he saw behind what appeared to be a posed smile. His eyes seemed lost—or rather sad—and piteously empty in some all-encompassing, life-restraining context. In contrast, Mark saw genuine love and affection in the face of Samantha, as she posed close by Thomas' side.

"That particular photograph was taken the summer before he died," she continued. "Actually, that's the last picture taken of me with my father."

"I can see where you get your beauty," Mark said without thinking. "He was a very distinguished looking gentleman."

Mark glanced at Sam and smiled. He could instantly tell that his compliment had embarrassed her, and at the same time, he realized that blushing became her. That revelation made his smile grow wider still. They held each other's gaze a second longer before Sam turned and walked over to one of the bookshelves.

"Well," she said as she retrieved one of the two old manila envelopes from a top shelf, "I'm sure you're anxious to see this. I know you have come a long way, and you have had an interest in this story for some time now. Do you think there really is a story here?"

"I'll certainly be in a better position to answer that question, as soon as I take a look," Mark replied, taking the envelope from Sam and sitting down on the couch that served as Sam's favorite reading spot. Sam allowed him her space and sat in an adjacent chair. She could tell she no longer had Mark's attention and retreated to the comfort of her wine and her own thoughts, as she watched him discover more about her father's love.

Mark looked at the old envelope. The moment he had been waiting for had finally arrived. He had been drawn to this moment by reasons he found hard to explain or understand.

Across the front of the envelope he saw the words "from Amanda" written in Thomas Kane's handwriting. Mark's fingers were almost trembling as he opened the clasp and pulled out the stack of papers sheltered inside the envelope. He picked up the first sheet and slowly began to read.

"I still can feel his tender touch,
So gentle on my skin.
He's taken me to places where
Few lovers have ever been.

I lie and watch him sleeping now;
I softly caress his hair.
He turns and smiles in his sleep;
Does he know how much I care?

If my love for him in words be told,
Then this I would decree:
The only sorrow I ever feel
Is for those who are not me.

I often wonder as I watch him sleep,
Is it me he's dreaming of?
Does he dream of our lives together,
A life so full of love?

But I awoke and knew the dream's not his.
Once again the day began
With my realizing as I do each day:
I'm with another man."

In reading the first of Amanda's poems, it became evident to Mark why Thomas and Amanda did not end up together. Amanda was obviously married at the time. On the surface, one might assume this to be a classic affair of the heart. However, Mark knew from his reading of Thomas Kane's love for this woman that this was turning out to be more of a tragic and thwarted affair of the soul.

Mark looked up into Sam's eyes. She simply gave him a smile without saying a word. He looked back at the envelope and picked up the next page from the stack of poems.

" Together, our hopes will stand as one.
Between us, a single aim.
Together, we'll search for ways to grow,
And never look for blame.

Together, we'll listen to concerns
That each to the other has spoken.
Together, we'll encourage each others dreams,
With mutual support unbroken.

Together, between us, a single truth,
With neither telling lies.
Together, because of the way we care,
We'll each become more wise.

Together, we'll bury the pain of the past,
Our goal being that of winning.
Together, our love will always survive,
With each day a new beginning.

Together, we'll fit like no one else,
With neither being master.
Together, we'll share all things in life,
From triumph through disaster."

Mark found himself curious with regard to the chronology of the writings. Like Thomas Kane's words, none of Amanda's writings bore any reference to when they had been written. Understanding the order of what each had written to the other would have to wait until Mark could locate Amanda. She would be able to answer this and much more. As he selected another to read, Mark knew in his heart that finding Amanda was imperative to writing this story.

"Happiness has an endearing taste
That the sad can never know.
Loneliness is a bitter cold feeling
Of dark and empty woe.

Love is a gift that two together
Can share and become as one.
One alone is a ship without sails,
A victory never won.

Two can build on countless dreams,
And reach the highest star.
One is an endless winding road,
A goal forever far.

Together dreams become reality,
A security forever lasting.
Alone is perpetual infinity,
A soul forever grasping."

Mark could sense a deep measure of sadness and regret in Amanda's words. It was almost as though Amanda somehow knew that in spite of her love for Thomas, she would never be free of the bonds that kept her from him.

Mark continued to read what Amanda had written, one poem after another. While some of her words held the promise that she would someday be with Thomas, most projected a message of resignation filled with anguish and utter woe.

"Alone and tired, my heart gave way;
I played my memory again.
For me, it seemed the only way
To live with what has been.

I remembered that feelings of love are more
Than words could ever say.
I'd trade in all my love to come
For a single yesterday.

But all the days my future holds
Are nights without an end.
And as I cried my thousandth tear,
You asked to be my friend.

I looked into your eyes so bright,
And was lost amidst your charm.
You seemed to say with a single glance
You'd never cause me harm.

You gently touched me with your hand;
You said you really cared.
I found myself confiding in you
Those thoughts I'd never shared.

With each passing day you are there,
I need you more and more.
But if love can't last forever and a day,
Then what's forever for?

Still, if I were to believe, as some often do,
That I've lived a life before,
I'd want to believe it was you I loved,
On some far and distant shore."

Some of Amanda's poems were quite short, as though the
act of writing down her feelings was simply too hard to do.

"In awakening comes my morning stretch;
Shaking sleep's web of dew.
The first thoughts in my foggy mind
Are thoughts of loving you.

I drink my coffee, I read the news,
I shower, and wash my hair.
Yet no matter what I seem to do,
In my mind you're always there.

But when I look into the mirror,
It's me alone I see.
I hope no matter where you are,
You're still in love with me."

Another of Amanda's poems deeply touched Mark. While short in words, it was infinitely deep in meaning.

"With every moment we're apart
I miss your loving touch.
I've promised to you the world and more...
I love you, oh, so much.

My life is empty without your smile,
Your smell, your voice, and such.
The room still echoes your words to me:
"I love you, oh, so much."

While still another simply read:

"You said you wished I'd write a poem
To tell you why I'm blue.
Quite simply, my love, the reason is
I'm so in love with you."

It took Mark almost an hour to carefully read all twenty-eight of Amanda's writings. He reverently placed the poems back into the old manila envelope that had sheltered them over the years and took his first drink of the wine Sam had brought him an hour before.

Mark looked at Sam, who had been patiently awaiting his response. He could tell she was anxious to know his thoughts.

"Samantha," he slowly began, "I am still not sure why this story has captivated my interest and imagination, but it has. And now, it was done so even more, now that I have read what Amanda wrote to your father. I believe in my heart there is a story in all of this—especially if I can locate Amanda. She remains the key to our understanding the whole story. With your help, I'd like to undertake an all-out effort to locate Amanda."

Mark immediately saw that his willingness to pursue the story pleased Samantha. Her eyes seemed to brighten as she gave him an approving smile. It was becoming obvious to him that Samantha was as helplessly drawn to this as he knew himself to now be.

"Mark," Sam said with obvious conviction, "I'd very much like to help you find Amanda."

Chapter Thirteen

he next morning, Mark arrived at Samantha's just before 9:00 AM. They had agreed to meet over breakfast and plan their strategy for locating Amanda. Sam had given a copy of Amanda's writings to Mark as he left her house the night before, and he had spent an additional two hours in his hotel room carefully re-reading each one. Yet for all his effort, Mark was unable to find any clue to Amanda's identity or whereabouts. Consequently, he was not really sure how to proceed.

Sam greeted Mark at the door with mock surprise.

"Good morning, stranger!" she said facetiously. "I haven't seen you for ages."

Mark gave her his famous Benton smile.

"Good morning, Samantha." he said, following Sam into her bright, sunny kitchen. "I hope you didn't go to a lot of trouble this morning. Coffee would be just fine." He could tell from the inviting smell, however, she had gone to a lot of trouble.

"It was no trouble," Sam replied, gesturing for Mark to take a seat at the table. "I figured you to be a person who would be prompt, so I have breakfast ready to go. Since I wasn't exactly sure how you liked your eggs, I went with scrambled. Everyone likes scrambled, right?"

Mark looked at the food Sam had placed on the table. In addition to scrambled eggs, there was bacon, sausage, southern-style white gravy, hash brown potatoes, toast, juice, and coffee. He had not had a home-cooked breakfast made especially him since his mother died. Of course, he was not counting his daily breakfast at Mandy's Café as being 'home-cooked.'

"Wow," was all he could say in response. "I'm not used to any kind of special treatment. As a matter of fact, I'm more accustomed to eating breakfast while being ragged on by a bunch of cantankerous old fools."

"I can promise I won't be cantankerous," Sam assured him, "but I can't say I won't act a little foolish with you at my table."

Sam immediately wished she had kept her comment to herself. It was not like her to show an interest in a man—as if the huge meal she had spent the last hour preparing was not an outward show of interest! However, when their eyes briefly met, she was suddenly glad she had said it. Mark's eyes seemed to admit that he, too, felt a little foolish around her, in a charming yet boyish sort of way.

The two enjoyed breakfast, conversation, and afterward, sunshine, fresh air, and another cup of coffee on the patio. Even though they had spent, in total, little more than six hours together, Samantha Kane and Mark Benton already knew much about each other's life. They shared many similar interests, along with a common willingness to try new things and an inherent passion for travel and adventure. Clearly, they both realized that some sort of relationship was developing between the two of them, and it seemed neither of them wanted to prevent it from happening.

"Samantha," Mark finally said, bringing their conversation to the issue of Amanda for the first time that day, "I spent a couple more hours last night trying to learn something—

anything—from Amanda's writings. Unfortunately, I simply couldn't find any clues."

"I know," agreed Sam. "I've looked for clues on more than one occasion, but there just aren't any to be found—at least, not in her writings."

Mark sensed there was more to her last statement than the obvious.

"What do you mean," he asked, "by 'not in her writings'?"

"Well, I'm not sure what, if anything, can be learned from this," she said, "but I recently found out from my mother that she had a short conversation with a woman named Amanda a couple of months after my father died."

With that single statement, Sam had Mark's undivided attention, as she recounted the story her mother had recently shared. Sam described how Amanda had mailed a letter to her father, only to have it returned as "undeliverable." She further told Mark how a severe snowstorm had brought down telephone lines in the Preston Falls area that winter.

"I remember that storm," Mark interjected, recalling to himself how they had also gone without electricity for nearly a week after that storm.

Sam explained how Amanda had seemed extremely anxious to talk to her father, but had not given her mother a reason why. Then, upon learning of her father's death, how Amanda had hung up the telephone, without saying another word and without ever calling her mother again.

"You're right," Mark said. "The only thing Amanda's call to your mother proves is that she did, in fact, exist and that she was alive at that time. Do you know if Amanda spoke with any discernable accent?"

"I asked that question," Sam answered, "but my mother said she didn't notice anything specific in her voice or her accent."

"We can probably assume another thing," Mark said, as he continued to conjecture. "Amanda must not have been in constant contact with your father."

"How do you figure?" Sam asked.

"Well," explained Mark, "why was it that, in December, Amanda was still unaware of your father's death in October?"

Sam nodded. "I see your point," she said in agreement. "That might help explain why, when I packed up my father's things, I found no letters from Amanda."

"How do you figure?" Mark asked, trying to understand Sam's logic.

"Well," Sam continued, "take, for example, Amanda's poems. They are all neatly typed. Speaking as a woman, I do not think Amanda would have typed and mailed them each time. A woman would be more apt to handwrite poems to her lover."

"And if she had," Mark added, "I would think that a man—especially a man living by himself—would keep them."

"Exactly," said Sam, "which would mean they should have been among my father's things, but they weren't. So, I've been thinking that they might have stayed in contact via a different medium—say, e-mail."

Mark thought for a moment about that possibility.

"That would explain," he slowly agreed, "why Amanda's poems were typed. Your father could simply cut and paste the words electronically from her e-mails to his word processor and then print them. It is just too bad we no longer have the option of looking at his computer at work, which would now be long gone. I'll bet Amanda's e-mail address was right there in his electronic address book."

Sam suddenly straightened her posture in a manner that caught Mark's attention.

"What is it, Samantha?" he asked, sensing he had just witnessed a personal epiphany.

"Well, after all these years, I certainly can't speak to the whereabouts of my father's computer at Mountain View College," Sam said. "However, I do have his personal laptop computer."

Mark now caught his own breath. The possibilities of what might be learned from Thomas Kane's personal laptop seemed endless. Sam sensed his sudden excitement and quickly spoke again.

"Well, before you get too excited," she warned, "I have already looked at all the files on his laptop—several times, in fact. I can assure you there are no files anywhere on the hard drive that would shed light on Amanda's identity or her whereabouts. I have gone through all of his saved documents and found nothing. I have gone through his saved e-mails and found nothing. If my father saved anything from Amanda, it must have been on his desktop computer at work, where he had access to a printer, since he did not have a printer at home."

"Then why your sudden excitement a moment ago?" asked Mark, now somewhat confused by her initial reaction.

"Because," Sam answered excitedly, as she rose from her patio chair, "I just realized I never checked his e-mail address book!"

Sam jumped up and left the room, leaving Mark alone only for a moment. When she returned, she was carrying her father's old laptop case. Together, they spent the next few minutes removing the aging computer from the case and plugging the charger cord into the machine—a clear sign the battery was no longer any good.

"How old is this thing?" Mark asked, as he watched in agony. Without a doubt, he was witnessing the slowest boot sequence he had seen in years.

"This laptop is probably at least ten years old," she replied. "It's like watching paint dry!"

Mark laughed aloud, appreciating with each hour he spent with Samantha her wonderful sense of humor. After several excruciating moments more, the computer was up and ready. As Mark sat next to her and watched, Sam opened what appeared to be one of the first versions of a now obsolete e-mail software program. She navigated through the program menus with flawless intuitiveness and soon had the address book displayed on the screen. Across the top read the words "57 records." They both could see that the addresses appeared in no discernable order, so Sam began cycling through each record.

With each record viewed, Sam commented to Mark "that is a cousin," or, "that was an old friend," or, at times, "I'm not sure who that is." Still, they found what they were looking for after only a dozen or so records. It read "amandaj@inet. services.com." There was no other information available.

"Amanda J.," Mark read aloud. "Well, it certainly begs the question of whether 'J' represents her middle name or her last name. Moreover, what is "inet.services.com?" I've never heard of them."

Sam turned off the computer and put it back into its case, while Mark returned to his chair.

"They were one of the first ISP's in this country," she answered.

"ISP's?" asked Mark.

"Sorry," Sam replied, suddenly realizing that Mark was not as close to technology as she was. "Internet service provider's—companies that offer e-mail service and Internet access for a monthly fee."

"Well, there you go," Mark said, anxious to use this newfound information. "Let's give them a call and ask about Amanda J."

"Slow down, cowboy," Sam said with less enthusiasm than Mark was exhibiting. "I can see two problems right off the bat. First, ISP's will not release any information about their customers except when directed to do so by court order. And I'm relatively certain our inquisitiveness is insufficient reason to obtain a court order."

She could see the immediate disappointment in Mark's face.

"And," she continued, "if that weren't reason enough to scrap your plan, then how about this: INET.SERVICES. COM ceased to exist over two years ago as a result of one of those huge dot-COM mergers."

Mark's newfound hope was going down in flames. He was beginning to think the mystery of Amanda's identity was destined to stay just that—an unsolved mystery.

"I need to find Amanda and talk to her!" Mark said in exasperation. "How am I ever going to be able to write about something I know so very little about?"

"I know," Sam offered sympathetically. "Believe me, I need to find answers as badly as you do—albeit for different reasons. Not that it makes much of a difference now, but I need to know if this woman was the reason our family fell apart years ago."

Mark had been thinking about finding Amanda for months, but it was becoming apparent he was no closer to finding her now than he was in the beginning. He simply did not know what to do next.

"There is one other thing," Sam said, breaking the silence that had fallen between them.

"Yes?" he replied in a monotone that reflected his sense of defeat.

"There's something I want to show you," she continued. "It's in the living room."

Mark followed Sam into the living room. He watched as she retrieved a small object from the top shelf of a bookcase. She placed in his hand the petite picture frame that roughly measured three inches by two inches. Neatly pressed under the frame's glass was a small flower—a violet. As he handed back the violet, Mark looked to Sam for an explanation.

"I guess I should start at the beginning," she said.

"That's always a good place to start," agreed Mark.

"Well," she slowly began, "I made a promise of sorts at my father's funeral three years ago. I promised him—or promised myself, I suppose—that I would return on the anniversary of his death each year, to pay my respects and reaffirm the love I'll always have in my heart for him."

"So you've gone back, then, each year?" Mark asked.

"So far," Sam replied, "I have lived up to that promise. I always go by myself each year; my mother has never been— not that I expect her to."

Sam looked at the framed violet and quickly became lost in thought. Watching her, Mark found himself thinking several things at once. He thought how incredibly beautiful

Samantha Kane was, especially with the sun striking her the way it was at that particular moment. He also thought something significant was about to be said, since Samantha was taking time to reflect before she spoke. Mark felt his impatience begin to rise, but made himself wait in silence until she was ready to resume her story.

"Anyway," she continued after a few moments, "last October, I made my annual visit to the cemetery. After parking the car, I walked toward his grave. Then, I noticed something lying across the top of the gravestone. As I drew closer, I could see it was a bouquet of freshly cut violets."

"Violets?" asked Mark, recalling that in the poetry, there were numerous references to violets.

"Yes," Sam confirmed, holding up the small frame for him to see. "This is one of those violets."

Mark felt hope rise within him once again. He wondered why she had not told him about this discovery sooner. The origin of the flowers seemed all too obvious.

"Samantha," he said, "there is little doubt in my mind who placed those violets on your father's grave."

Sam, however, was not so quick to agree.

"At one point," she conceded, "I thought they must be from Amanda. However, after I thought it through, I found myself less sure."

"Why?" Mark asked.

"Well," she continued, "it makes no sense that the flowers showed up three years after his death. As I said, I visited my father's grave each year and there was no sign of flowers the previous years. If the bouquet was from Amanda, I suppose I could understand the significance, but I certainly don't understand the timing."

Mark took the violet from Sam, walked to the living room window, and closely examined the flower in the brighter sunlight, as though a closer inspection might yield some latent clue to its origin. However, the only thought that came to Mark's mind was the simple yet pure beauty of the violet. He remembered thinking the same thought recently while looking at violets growing wild on the Mountain View College campus.

Nevertheless, Sam brought up a good point. If the flowers were from Amanda, why wait until the third anniversary of Thomas Kane's death to bring them? Why wouldn't Amanda have come sooner? It did not make a lot of sense. After all, Samantha made the trip every year.

And with that thought, Mark suddenly spun around to Samantha and asked, "You go to the cemetery every year, right?"

"Yes," Sam replied, her attention now caught by Mark's new tone.

"You go on the anniversary of his death, right?" Mark asked, seeking methodical confirmation of what she had already told him earlier.

"Yes." Sam could not see where he was going with these questions.

"On the exact anniversary date?" he asked, heavily enunciating the word 'exact.'

Mark's last question drew immediate silence, as Sam had to stop and think about the exact dates of her visits.

"Well," she finally replied, "Dad died on October 23rd, 1996. A year later, I made my first trip. It takes me about twelve hours to drive from here to Horton Grove, Illinois. What I do is leave early on a Saturday morning and make it there just before dark that night. I visit the gravesite, then I spend the night in a quaint little bed-and-breakfast nearby. I get up early the next morning, leave for home, and roll in here just before dark on Sunday night."

"Did you do the same thing each of your three trips?" Mark asked.

"Yes," Sam replied, "as a matter of fact I did."

It was not until Mark asked the next question that Sam finally saw where he was going with all this.

"Do you have an electronic calendar?" he asked.

It just so happened that Sam's cell phone was lying on the coffee table beside them. She picked it up and began pressing keys before Mark could ask the next question.

"Okay," Sam said, "the first year—1997—the weekend I went was October 18th and 19th, with the exact anniversary not until Thursday the 23rd."

Sam continued pressing keys.

"The second year," she continued, "was 1998. That year, I went up on Saturday, October 17th, and returned on Sunday the 18th. The anniversary of Dad's death was later that week—Friday, the 23rd."

Mark could bet what Sam was going to say next. She again tapped the screen a few times and confirmed what he suspected.

"Last year," she said, "I made the trip on Saturday, October 23rd—the exact date of his death!"

Sam and Mark looked at each other in disbelief, as the answer became obvious. It had suddenly made perfect sense. After months of trying to solve the mystery of Amanda's whereabouts, they both now realized they finally had her— or at least, it would seem they would have her on October 23rd.

"Amanda is probably going to the cemetery every year," Sam said triumphantly. "I visited before the anniversary date the first two trips, so I would not have seen her. I must have just missed her the last time I was there!"

"That would be my guess," Mark nodded in agreement. "And she is bringing your father the violets he loved so much.

Preston Falls was experiencing what was called an Indian summer, which, given the severity of the previous winter, was a much appreciated phenomenon. The temperature was in the upper sixties and the weather was supposed to be great for the upcoming week. Even though it was the second Saturday in October, Mark Benton had opened his windows at home and was enjoying the warm, fresh air. He had finished grading student essays and exams earlier that morning and was now sitting in his favorite chair, once again reading the words Thomas and Amanda's had written to one another.

It seemed every time he read them, what he considered to be his 'favorites' would change. Depending upon his mood at the time, the words would affect him in different ways. Now that Mark had met and spent time with Samantha, the stories of love lost were touching his heart in a way he had never before known—especially the words that Thomas had written.

"The days are meaningless hours on end;
The nights are dreadfully long.
I've given so much of my strength to you,
I'm no longer strong.

I need you now like never before;
Of this you can be sure:
I'm slowly dying a lonely death,
And you're the only cure.

At first, I thought I'd still go out,
And dance your memory away.
But soon the record began to skip,
With each additional play.

Yes, I played our song many times,
And danced the night away.
But the price of finding someone new
Was more than I could pay.

I knew all along my love was yours,
And no one else would do.
I could never give my heart away...
It still belongs to you."

Still another one of Thomas' poems read:

"I sat alone by a stream today,
And thought of days gone by.
I remembered those who touched my life;
I thought of you and cried.

Each tear I shed had something to say
Of the love I'd felt for you.
But each was washed quickly away
In the water cold and blue.

I guess that life is give and take
In all I see and find.
For with everything a man acquires,
There's something left behind.

It's sad that you can't be with me
As my dreams of life unfold.
For they, without you by my side,
Can't ever be fully told."

Mark set Thomas' writings aside and began looking through what Amanda had written. There were so many unanswered questions about Thomas and Amanda's relationship. Above all else was the question of 'why?'—why didn't a love as pure as theirs survive? Mark pondered that question as he read more of what Amanda had written.

"Raindrops falling on a house of glass,
Singing their songs of gloom,
Are slow to wash away the past
Of the lonely child of the womb.

She sits alone, afraid to speak,
Unaware of eventual doom
Which seeks and preys on the tired and weak:
This lonely child of the womb.

She reaches out, but nothing is there;
Her dreams lay scattered and strewn.
Her only hope is for someone to care
For a lonely child of the womb.

But the pain that life has thrown her way
Has forever sealed her tomb.
And no one takes the time to pray
For the lonely child of the womb."

There seemed such undeniable sadness in much of what Amanda had written. While a few of her poems celebrated the love she felt for Thomas, most seemed to be the result of her not being able to be with him.

"The words came out 'I love you'
As I whispered in his ear.
But the memory of you came back again,
And I fought another tear.

I felt the need I'd known before,
As we shared a warm embrace.
Yet when he turned to look at me,
I saw your loving face.

He said that with each passing day,
He loves me more and more.
And although for him, the feeling's real,
I've heard the words before.

He said he wants to share with me,
The things he's never tried.
But the desires I've given birth in him,
For me have long since died.

He wants to share a part of me
That you weren't able to take.
I find I want to call his name
'Bright Eyes' by mistake.

He hopes that I will give to him
The secrets of my heart.
But you alone have taken them,
As we spend our lives apart.

He says he wants me for all time,
With his love as my reward.
Yet the price he asks for me to pay
Is more than I can afford.

The words came out 'I love you'
As he whispered in my ear...
But the only love I'll ever know
Is a love no longer near."

'So many questions,' Mark thought. Still, if all went as planned, the answers were only a little more than a week away. He was flying to St. Louis, Missouri, next Tuesday morning on October 22nd. There, he would meet Samantha Kane, and together they would drive to Horton Grove, Illinois.

They had decided last summer during his Houston visit to make this trip together. The two had been in constant contact with each other since then planning out the details. During these past few months, Mark and Sam had grown closer to each other and both were looking forward to their reunion—and for more reasons than finding and speaking with Amanda.

The last time they spoke together on the telephone, Mark had mentioned how much he liked talking with Samantha. She, too, had admitted harboring the same feeling and remarked how ironic it was that the writings of two individuals who never ended up together were actually bringing the two of them together. Whatever the forces were, Mark only knew he was counting the hours before he would see Samantha again.

Chapter Fourteen

am arrived at the St. Louis airport an hour before Mark's afternoon flight was scheduled to land. She had left Houston early that morning and had driven straight through to the Gateway City. Now, as she sat and watched an endless stream of planes taxi then park and people come and go, the voice inside her head returned.

Isn't this what you wanted?

'I don't know what I want,' she thought, in conversation with the voice.

Yes, you do. You want answers. You want closure.

She was standing near the back of the waiting crowd as he exited the jet way into the terminal. When their eyes met, both smiled warmly to the other. Mark walked up to Samantha, dropped his bag, and gave her a more-than-casual hug, which she reciprocated by giving the same in return. While his arms were still around her, and before he had time to think about it, Sam gave him a gentle kiss on the lips.

You want him.

"It is really good to see you again," she said, still smiling as she looked into his eyes.

"Same goes for me," he assured her. "Since I knew I'd only be staying one night, I traveled light. I have everything right here with me."

"Great," Sam said. "Did you get confirmation on your return flight?"

Mark pulled the ticket from inside his jacket pocket.

"My flight leaves at 10:40 tomorrow night," he said, reading from his itinerary. "How much of a drive is it to Horton Grove from here?"

"About two hours," she replied. "We should plan on leaving there tomorrow evening by 6:00 PM, just to be safe."

"Sounds like a plan," Mark said, reaching down for his bag. "Are you ready for this?"

Sam took a deep breath and replied, "As ready as I'll ever be, I suppose!"

Taking his bag with one hand and her hand with the other, Mark walked out of the terminal with Sam. Within minutes they had found her car in the sea of vehicles neatly parked in the short-term parking garage. Sam paid the gate attendant as they exited, and they soon found themselves crossing the Mississippi River into what the welcome sign called 'The Great State of Illinois.'

As they made their way along Illinois Route 492 East, traveling from one small town to the next, conversation between them jumped from one topic to another. Before they knew it, the two hours passed unannounced and they found themselves entering the small town of Horton Grove.

"You know," Sam said, as she glanced from side to side, "this town still looks the same as it did when I came here as a young girl."

"I think small towns have a way of staying the same," Mark replied. "It's almost as though they were meant to exist in their own little world and in their own time, regardless of any external forces."

Sam slowed the car to a stop. They had arrived at Horton Grove's one-and-only four-way stop sign. To the right was downtown, a one-block collection of early 20th century buildings housing everything from Ted March's clothing store to Ben Elliot's grocery. It was after five o'clock, so the only shops still open were Bob's Barber Shop located on the corner next to them and Evelyn's 5¢ & 10¢ Store, which for years had been referred to locally as the 'Five and Dime.' Both displayed signs in their windows that read OPEN UNTIL SIX.

Sam turned left, then immediately pulled into the driveway of a large, older home. A small sign in the yard read Mentone Bed & Breakfast, and hanging below it was a smaller sign that read VACANCY.

'I'll bet that VACANCY sign has never been changed,' Mark thought, as he looked around the small community.

"Well, this is it," Sam said and turned off the engine of her Mercedes. "This is the hotel I told you about. I stay here every year. Dave & Claudia Mentone are wonderful people and they always take very good care of me. Let's go inside and I'll introduce you."

Clearly, Sam was excited to see her old acquaintances once again. Before the two of them made it halfway up the porch steps, a smiling, elderly couple came out the front door and onto the porch to greet them.

"Samantha!" Dave said, quickly giving Sam a hug.

"It's so good to see you again," Claudia chimed in, also giving Sam a hug.

"It's good to see you both!" Sam replied with genuine enthusiasm. "I'd like you to meet my friend, Mark Benton. Mark is a college professor and a writer."

Suddenly, Mark was being welcomed in the same fashion as Sam. They were then led into the residence-turned-hotel. Dave saw to it they both were properly registered, and Claudia showed them both to their separate rooms. Mark was relieved to find the owner's initial friendliness did not lead to a pull-up-a-chair-and-let's-talk situation, since he was hoping to spend every free minute talking with Sam.

Dave and Claudia were not from Horton Grove. Dave was a retired dentist from back East and the two of them had moved here six years earlier. They had bought the old Bradshaw place left empty after the widow Carey Bradshaw died. The Mentone's converted this unique, seven-bedroom house into a quaint bed and breakfast hotel. Consequently, their only concern was to be as friendly and accommodating as possible, without infringing upon the privacy of their guests.

Mark removed the clothes from his bag and hung them in the closet. He placed his toiletries in the small bathroom adjacent to his bedroom, then went down the hall to Sam's room. He gently knocked on her door.

When Sam opened the door, Mark smiled boyishly and said, "I noticed they have a porch swing. Would you like to go outside and sit for a little while?"

Sam gave Mark a smile and stepped out into the hall. She was already holding a sweater.

"I was just getting ready to ask you the same thing!" she replied.

"You know," Mark said, as he helped her put on the sweater, "I don't think I've ever seen so many doilies in one place."

Sam laughed as they walked down the front stairs and out onto the porch.

"You have to admit," Sam said, "they do make you feel as though you are in a very special place."

"I suppose they do," Mark conceded aloud, while thinking 'if you consider being in doily hell a special place!' Then, with a famous Benton smile sent her way, Mark escorted Sam to the front porch, where they sat down together on an oversized white swing.

For the first few minutes, neither of them spoke. The dusk seemed filled with the sound of chirping crickets and an occasional locust. Mark and Sam both seemed content for the moment to simply listen to the world around them and to watch as fireflies began their evening dance.

Mark made the swing move in constant yet gentle rhythm. Sam finally spoke first.

"Mark," she began, "I'm a little scared."

"About tomorrow?" he asked. Seeing Samantha as less than the confident woman he was growing to know was something new.

"Yes," she said. "I guess I'm not sure what I'll say to Amanda, if she does in fact show up."

"Just tell her who you are," Mark told her, reaching for her hand, "and I'm sure the conversation will happen naturally from that point."

"What are you hoping to accomplish tomorrow?" asked Sam, content to leave her hand in his.

Mark slowly brought the swing to a stop, as he thought about his answer.

"I will want to show her the poems," he said finally. "Then, I guess I'll tell her I'd like to write a story about the two of them. She will probably want some time to think about it. So, I guess I'm hoping to at least initiate a line of communication, whereby I can contact her in the weeks to come."

The sounds of crickets continued to fill the evening air. Once again, Mark started the gentle motion of the swing. Sam could not remember ever feeling as safe and secure as she did at that moment. Together, they sat in the swing for another hour. They talked some, but mostly, they just listened to the night, to the sound of the old swing, and for those few moments together, they listened to their hearts.

But is was the voice inside Sam that insisted upon having the last word as they retired to their rooms for the night.

The answer is right in front of you. He is your answer.

The next morning, Mark found Sam waiting for him downstairs at the breakfast table. As he sat down, he thought how he had never seen Samantha looking so beautiful. Her hair was down, falling loosely on her shoulders. Her smile was absolutely radiant.

"Good morning," he said to her, just as Claudia breezed into the room from the adjoining kitchen. "And, good morning to you, Claudia."

"Now, you two don't mind me—I think this is the last of it," Claudia said, as she set a tray of preserves among everything else already on the table.

"Thanks, Claudia," Sam told her, "and tell Dave thanks, too. I suspect he still does most of the cooking."

"I still make him do all the cooking," Claudia happily reported. Then, having said that, she breezed out of the room in the same manner she had entered, leaving the two of them alone to enjoy their breakfast. Given the variety of food prepared, they both took advantage of the situation and enjoyed a great home-style meal.

Within the hour, Sam and Mark had finished breakfast. They said their thanks and their goodbyes to Dave and Claudia Mentone and were soon in the parking lot preparing to leave.

"I need to go by the local flower shop first," Sam told Mark, "and pick up a rose."

"Of course," Mark replied without any further discussion. He was sensitive to the fact that a part of this trip was more than investigative—that Samantha would be paying respect to her father's memory.

Sam drove a block down Main Street and parked in front of a small gift shop. Once inside, Mark saw that one corner of the store also served as a flower shop. Sam asked a middle-aged woman who was tending the store to prepare her a single red rose. While the clerk prepared the flower, Mark spoke up.

"Do you sell violets?" he asked, giving Sam a knowing look.

"Violets?" the woman repeated. "No, that's not a flower we'd have much demand for around here. Shoot, even if we did, I am not sure I have ever seen violets listed on our supplier's inventory. I doubt they would even be available."

Her answer was not the answer he wanted to hear. "Are you sure?" he asked, pressing the woman to think hard.

"Well, I can call if you'd like," the clerk replied.

"No," said Mark. "That won't be necessary. I was just curious, that's all."

Sam paid for the rose and they walked outside to the car. The sky was becoming more overcast, as clouds began to hide the early morning sun. It was common for the skies to be gray this time of the year, even with no rain in the forecast.

"Well, I was hoping for some information," Mark confessed. "But, it appears that Amanda is bringing the violets with her, if she is the one placing them on your father's grave."

"It would seem that way," agreed Sam, as they got back into the car. She started up the engine and within minutes, they were turning off the main highway onto the well-traveled, one-lane road that cut through the heart of the old cemetery. The time was just past 9:30 AM.

"You know," she said, driving slowly through the cemetery, "we may have to wait here all day."

"Well," Mark replied, "let's hope Amanda doesn't keep us waiting too long."

Nevertheless, Mark knew Sam was right. It might very well be a long wait. Before retiring the night before, he had asked Dave Mentone if there was a woman named Amanda registered at the hotel. But Dave had assured him they were the only two guests that night. All indications were that Amanda would be arriving sometime during the course of the day.

Sam drove the car past the older graves located near the entrance and brought the car to a stop near the back of the cemetery. Everything was just as she remembered.

"My father's grave is near that old oak tree," Sam said, pointing to the tree on her left. They got out of the car together, but Mark remained behind, allowing Sam to first visit the grave alone. He watched as she walked to the gravesite, recalling how he felt each time he visited the graves of his parents.

Sam stood beside her father's gravestone and looked at the words. Thomas Randall Kane. Born November 19, 1941. Died October 23, 1996. It didn't say much. But in the end, what more was there to say? A man lived and a man died. Perhaps it should also say that he loved and that he was loved. By loving, a person's life is not lived in vain. At least, that's what Sam wanted to believe.

For the first time since his death, she was filled with much that needed to be said. She sat down on the brown, autumn grass next to her father's gravestone.

"Hi, Daddy," Sam said in a soft voice. "I've brought someone that I wish you could have met. He is smart and, oh, such a gentleman. His name is Mark Benton, and he teaches at Mountain View. You would have really liked him—he tells me he is a big fan of the Washington Redskins. You always said that was a prerequisite for your liking any boy I dated, remember? Anyway, his parents are both gone and he spends as much time helping others as he can.

"I haven't told him yet, Daddy, but I am in love with him. And you should know it was you who brought us together. He found the poems you wrote to Amanda in an envelope behind a file cabinet. Then, he found me in an attempt to learn more about the love you felt for Amanda. Yes, Daddy,

I know about Amanda. I found the poems she wrote to you among your things. I know I have never talked about her, but, today, I hope to meet her. It has been her—she is the one who has been bringing you the violets, isn't she?"

Sam leaned over to brush away some of the old oak tree's leaves from around the base of her father's gravestone.

"By meeting Amanda I hope to learn more about you. And in doing so, I might learn more about myself. When I first found the poems in your office, I couldn't understand the meaning behind Amanda's words. It was so hard for me to picture you loving someone I had never met. But since I met Mark, I know exactly how you both must have felt. And by knowing that feeling myself, I can now accept her in my life. I look forward to meeting her, Daddy. I'm anxious to know the woman who meant so much to you."

Sam stood and placed the rose on the grave.

"Goodbye, Daddy. Please continue to watch over me. Just because you are gone does not mean I can live without you. And just because I've found someone to love the way you loved Amanda doesn't mean he will ever replace the love I have for you."

Sam turned and looked back at Mark. Without her saying a word, Mark knew this was his cue to join her. He walked over to the grave and Sam put her arm around him. He looked for the first time at the grave of Dr. Thomas Kane.

"My father," Sam said. "I wish you could have known him, Mark. I think the two of you would have got along famously."

Mark smiled at Sam and put his arm around her as well. He was about to tell her that he too wished the same, when suddenly a small brown van came over the hill behind them. The van, which bore no markings or advertisements, followed the narrow road and came to a stop behind Sam's parked car. A middle-aged man got out of the van. Carrying a small basket, he began coming toward them.

"Howdy, folks," the man said, as he walked up. "I couldn't help but notice your plates. Bet it's a lot warmer down in Texas than it is here!"

When neither Sam nor Mark spoke up right away, the man sensed he was intruding.

"I'm sorry," he said quickly. "I don't mean to intrude."

He reached into the basket and removed a beautiful bouquet of violets. He reverently placed them atop Thomas Kane's gravestone, turned, and headed back toward the van.

"Wait!" Mark called out. Both Sam and Mark quickly caught up with him.

"Yes?" the man said.

"Who are you?" Sam asked.

"Name's Art Miller," he replied.

"Why are you bringing violets to Thomas Kane's grave?" Mark asked.

"You folks knew Thomas Kane?" the man wanted to know.

"He's my father," Sam informed him. "Mr. Miller, why are you bringing flowers?"

"His daughter," echoed Mr. Miller. "You don't say. I just figured him to have no one but her, since I never saw any other wreaths on the grave."

"Her who?" asked Sam, her impatience starting to rise.

"The woman," he said. Mr. Miller looked at the two of them and saw the confusion on their faces. "You don't know about the woman, do you?"

"Not until you tell us," Mark countered.

"Well," Mr. Miller began. "It was around Christmas, about five years ago, that this woman comes into my store."

"Store?" asked Mark.

"I own and operate Miller's Flowers," he replied, "down in Carson. That is about 38 miles south of here. Anyway, the woman—Amanda Brice was her name—comes in and asks me about getting some violets. I tell her that violets are not that easy to get. Still, she insists, so I get on the phone to my supplier. I find out there is a source—down in Puerto Rico, of all places—where I can get violets. However, they would have to be flown into the closest airport. And a small arrangement would cost over a hundred dollars. Imagine that! Anyway, once she heard how much they would cost, I figured that would be the end of it.

"But instead, she thinks a minute, and then asks me what it would cost to have violets placed on a gravesite once each year in perpetuity. I said I did not know—I'd never been asked that question before. The next thing I know, she is taking out a wad of cash from her purse. After counting it all out, asks if I could do it for $3,240. I asked her if she was sure about this and she said she was. So, I said, 'Yes, I would see to it for that amount.' I figured, even with inflation, I could keep it going at least twenty-five years.

"Anyway, she paid the money and asked that the flowers be delivered to Thomas Kane's gravesite in the Horton Grove cemetery each year on October 23rd. And, well, I've been doing just that for four years now."

"Unbelievable!" Mark exclaimed. "We've been looking to meet her for some time now. We were really hoping to find her here today. I don't suppose you know where she is, do you?"

"As a matter of fact," Mr. Miller replied without hesitation, "I do."

He then turned and walked back towards Thomas Kane's grave. However, instead stopping there, he went directly to the grave adjacent Kane's. Mark and Sam walked up beside Mr. Miller. Their hearts jumped in unison. A simple stone marked the grave beside her father. It read Amanda J. Brice. Died December 18, 1996. There was no birth date given.

"She's here," he announced, "buried right here along side Mr. Kane."

The moment had suddenly become surreal. Neither Mark nor Sam could grasp what they were seeing and hearing.

"I... I don't understand," stammered Sam, desperately trying to make sense of it all.

"Well," Mr. Miller said, "the only reason I know the whole story is because the Wallace County sheriff came by to see me two days after this woman had been in my shop. It seems that after seeing me, she came back here to the cemetery, supposedly to pay her respects. But by the will of God Almighty, the woman dropped dead of a heart attack right here where we are standing—least ways, that's what the county coroner ruled.

"Anyway, the next day, someone called the sheriff—without leaving their name—to report a woman's body seen lying up here in the cemetery. When a deputy responded to the call, he found her lying here, and the contents of her purse were scattered about the ground around her. It seems her wallet and all her identification were missing. They never did turn up. The sheriff told me later he thought some kids probably found her dead and took her wallet. Makes you wonder what the world is coming to, doesn't it? Anyway, the reason the sheriff came to see me was because she still had a copy of the receipt for the flowers in her purse, which she had signed 'Amanda J. Brice.'

"They had the coroner investigate, to make sure there was no foul play, if you know what I mean. In the end, they ruled her death to be by natural causes."

"But why is she buried here?" Sam asked, still not quite grasping the complete story.

"Well," Mr. Miller continued, "it's like I said—other than her name on the receipt, there was no identification to be found. The sheriff ran a missing persons report in all fifty states, but he did not get a positive ID. My cousin Ben works at the newspaper in Carson and he told me they even sent off her fingerprints, but nowhere was a record or match found. And it seems she rode the bus into town, since no car registered to her was ever found.

"In the end, the only thing they had on her was her name and the story I told them about the flowers. After thirty days, with no one claiming her body, the county went ahead and buried her as an indigent transient. It was not until 1997, the first year I delivered flowers here, that I noticed the county had buried her right beside him. Kind of ironic, huh?

"Well, that's everything I know to tell. If you are still interested, you might check with the sheriff's office in town."

With the story now told, the florist turned and walked back to his van. Mark called after him, thanking him for sharing the story with them. Mr. Miller waved without turning, got into the van, and drove away. Sam stood in stunned silence, continuing to look at Amanda's grave. After a few moments, she turned to Mark.

"I want to speak to the sheriff," she said.

"I do, too," agreed Mark. "Maybe he has turned up something the florist doesn't know about."

In a matter of ten minutes, Mark and Sam had driven back into town and were talking with Bob McKenzie, the local sheriff. McKenzie confirmed everything the florist had told them. He assured Sam and Mark that his office had done everything possible to further identify the woman and to locate the next of kin, but their efforts had been to no avail.

Mark and Sam thanked him for his time and were about to leave, when the sheriff told them to wait a moment more. He went into a back room and returned a few moments later carrying a paper bag.

"It has been five years, and we've not received a response to any of our missing person's queries. You two are the only ones who have shown any interest whatsoever. Why don't you take her belongings?"

"Oh, I don't know," stammered Sam, not knowing what to say.

"Well," the officer said, "there really isn't anything of value here—a hairbrush, some makeup and such. Oh, and there is also a letter. Since she was buried in the clothes she was wearing, this is all that's left."

"A letter?" asked Sam.

"Yes, ma'am," the sheriff replied, "but it contained no names or addresses. Anyway, you are welcome to her things. I'll just need you to sign a claim form."

Three hours later, Sam and Mark were sitting at a table in the corner of the airport cocktail lounge a few steps from his gate. His flight was not for another hour. Sam had reservations at a nearby hotel for the evening and would leave for Houston early the next morning.

They had elected not to read the letter inside Amanda's purse while they were in Horton Grove, nor did they read it in the car. Now, as they looked at each other, they both knew the time was right. Sam pulled the folded letter from the purse where it had been for the last five years.

"Should you read it," Sam asked, "or should I?"

"Go ahead," Mark replied. "You know, if I were to guess, I'd say that it might very well be the letter she sent to your father a few weeks before she died—the letter that came back to her marked undeliverable."

"Well," Sam said with a heavy sigh, "there's only one way to find out."

She slowly unfolded the letter, noticing right away that the handwriting was not her father's, but that of a another hand. She began to read aloud.

My Dearest Tom,
I cannot begin to describe the love inside my heart I feel for you. Without a doubt, you have been so patient for so very long now. Still, you must know your love sustained me through all my times of heartache and indecision. I guess it's been our separation that finally showed me what you've tried to tell me all along... we were meant to be together, and in every

way imaginable. I know that now.

Tom, I left him four months ago. I did not want to tell you at the time, because I knew you would be so worried. I drew upon the strength you gave me over the years and I went through it all by myself. I found a small furnished apartment, and have been working hard to save a little money. Our divorce was no contest, since I agreed to leave him everything, and it only took ninety days to become final. I am finally free!

Since you moved to Colorado, my life has been nothing more than a litany of empty lies. You alone have taught me how to love. More importantly, you have taught me how to be loved. I miss you so much.

Now you know why you have not heard from me for several months. Thank you for the space and time you gave to me. You always knew I had to get to this point on my own and you never pushed too hard. I love you so much for that.

Tom, I now belong to you. Please tell me it is not too late. I promise you will never regret the love you have shown me, nor the wait you have endured.

All my love,

Always, and in all ways...

AJ

he cursor blinked steadily on Mark's computer. He took a deep breath and began. Since he had already decided on a title, he quickly typed the words:

Some Things Left Behind
a collection of poems

In the beginning, he had hoped there would be a story in all of this. But with Thomas and Amanda both gone, their story could never fully be told. Only the words written between the two of them could now be shared, and those who read the words would have to write their own story.

The next page was the dedication and Mark typed the words:

**for my wife, Samantha,
in every way imaginable**

It had been a little over a year since Sam had sat across from him at a table in a Midwest airport and had read to him Amanda's last letter to her father. As soon as she finished reading it, Mark knew he was never going to let love escape him the way it had escaped Amanda and Thomas. He proposed to Samantha on the spot and Sam had said yes. Six months later they were married, making Emily Kane the happiest woman in Texas.

Sam had insisted on moving to Preston Falls, as opposed to Mark's moving to Houston. She was able to continue her work with Paul at the same software firm, doing so from the comfort of her new home. At least, Sam tried to work between the endless visits from George Vogel, Bob Tyler, Martin Dobbs and others. They had quickly adopted Samantha as one of their own, making it a point to drop by at least once each week—and usually around lunchtime.

For the next hour, Mark thought about what he might say as an introduction to the collection. But for some reason, words escaped him. It was difficult for him to explain poems that took on different meanings each and every time he read them.

Finally, Mark decided a short introduction was all that would be needed.

The following collection of poems was written by Thomas Randall Kane and by Amanda J. Brice. They were written as a testament of their love for one another. This book should serve to remind us all that true love survives within our spirits, long after our physical presence is gone.

Mark looked at the poems scattered about his desk. He picked up one written by Amanda and began to read the words.

"I closed my eyes and felt your warmth;
I held you, oh, so tight.
I awoke to find that you're not here...
I miss your love tonight.

You said our love would never end,
A love the world could see.
Yet now you're gone, and I'm alone;
Please hear my final plea.

Of all the love this world will know,
Our love is second to none.
Why then have you left me since
Our lives have just begun?

So much is there for us to share,
Each moment like no other.
A thought, a smile, a touch, a kiss,
We've given to one another.

Regardless of what I said before,
I'm not sure why you've gone.
As long as I know our love exists,
I'll forever still hold on.

It will not matter what you do,
Or where you choose to go.
I'll love you until the day I die;
My heart can't let you go.

Always know I'll come for you,
No matter where you'll be.
When you hear a voice call out your name,
The voice belongs to me."

Mark set the poem aside and picked up another, this one written by Thomas.

"With everything a man acquires,
There's something left behind.
So often I try to understand
The price of what I find.

But I gladly leave my past behind,
And sincerely look to you
For the strength you're able to give to me:
A love that's real and true.

A love which makes the stars above
Brightly shine each night.
A love, when shared unselfishly,
Can make all things seem right.

It's because of this, I give to you
The pieces of my heart...
To hold, to mold, to care for until
Death would do us part."

"Sweetheart," Sam called from the kitchen, "supper's almost ready."

Mark laid the poem aside and walked into the kitchen, where he saw Sam setting plates on the table. He went to her and gave her a very long hug.

"What's become of you!" she asked, kissing her husband on the neck, while he held her tight.

"The only thing I've become," he softly whispered to Sam, "is extremely fond of you."